SHADOW DANCING

"It really is just about invisible." Grant was silent as he watched the tail rise into the air. "But you can see its shadow from up here looking down on it. How much longer can you keep us in the air?" Grant asked.

"That's anyone's guess," Oz told him. "Probably only a few more minutes before our transmission burns up. We've completely lost all our fluid."

"You're the pilot," Grant said. "You decide what we should do next."

"We ought to land. But we might cut them off before they get up to speed. What do you think?"

"Let's give 'em hell," Grant suggested.

Harper Paperbacks by
Duncan Long

Night Stalkers
Grim Reaper

Night
STALKERS
TWILIGHT JUSTICE

DUNCAN LONG

HarperPaperbacks
A Division of HarperCollinsPublishers

This is a work of fiction. The characters, incidents, and dialogues are products of the author's imagination and are not to be construed as real. Any resemblance to actual events or persons, living or dead, is entirely coincidental.

 HarperPaperbacks *A Division of* HarperCollins*Publishers*
10 East 53rd Street, New York, N.Y. 10022

Cover art by Edwin Herder

First printing: November 1990

Printed in the United States of America

HarperPaperbacks and colophon are trademarks of HarperCollins*Publishers*

10 9 8 7 6 5 4 3 2 1

For Jean and Bob

ACKNOWLEDGMENTS

I must once again extend my gratitude to Ethan Ellenberg who often helped "talk me through" and iron out a few of the plot hang-ups in this story. Thanks should go to my editors, Ed Breslin and Jessica Kovar, along with the staff at Harper Paperbacks who made another of the Night Stalkers books possible.

On the home front, Kristen and Nicholas have again helped out in keeping the wild things at bay. And my greatest gratitude must go Maggie who has patiently helped in everything from major plotting to catching a wealth of typos that crept into the first few drafts of this manuscript.

P R O L O G U E

The bony man pulled the collar of his coveralls together and shivered in the cool night air as he crossed the tarmac. A breeze whistled around the airplane hangar and kicked up a cloud of dust. The airborne grit threatened to lodge under the green contact lenses he wore to alter the color of his eyes.

Spying an armed French Fusiliers Commando de l'Air who advanced from around a corner of the building, the bony man flattened himself inside the dark shadows of the hangar doorway, hoping he hadn't been seen.

Holding his breath, the man felt like a fly waiting to be swatted. The sleepy French commando, whose duty it was to guard the airport, continued to trudge toward him, a FAMAS bullpup rifle slung haphazardly over his shoulder.

In the distance, toward Paris, the clouds flashed soundlessly with lightning, splashing the tarmac and hangar around the bony man with a flicker of brightness that, had the guard been alert, would have disclosed the intruder hiding in the doorway. The man's hand snaked toward the sharpened screwdriver concealed in the slit pocket on the leg of his coveralls.

But the soldier passed by, unaware of the intruder. In a few seconds, the commando had vanished into the night.

Satisfied he hadn't been seen, the man turned and inserted a pick gun into the lock of the door. He carefully twanged its trigger, releasing a spring inside the tool that slapped the pins within the lock. He expertly torqued the instrument against the pins as they bounced inside the lock. Within a few seconds, the pins were aligned; the lock turned smoothly, releasing the heavy bolt that had protected the door. He shoved the door ajar and quickly slipped through the opening.

Inside, the large hangar was empty except for the Sikorsky MH-60K "Special Operations Aircraft" in the center of the dimly-lit building. The black helicopter seemed small in the nearly cavernous hangar, even though it was over five meters high and almost 20 meters long from its tail to the rotor that stretched in front of its nose.

The man crossed the open floor toward the helicopter. At the nose of the aircraft, he paused to set down the red tool box he carried. He opened the box and extracted a small instrument. In another minute, he had released the hood at the nose of the helicopter to gain access to the electrical systems inside it.

After locating a specific cable, he reached back into his tool box and removed a small device and a pair of wire cutters. He then cautiously sliced into the cable; within moments he had mated the electronic device's wires to those of the cable.

He returned the wire cutters to the tool box and retrieved a metered instrument. This he employed to run a series of quick tests on the newly mounted device attached to the MH-60K's electrical system.

He wiped the electrical device clean of finger prints. Then he closed the hood of the helicopter and carefully wiped it clean as well.

The saboteur returned the instrument to the tool box, crossed the floor of the hangar, and left as quietly as he had come.

1

The MH-60K helicopter sped forward, nearly skimming the concrete below it. The chopper's shadow sprang away from the airfield as the huge machine leaped skyward so quickly that there was an audible gasp from the spectators crowded into the grandstand.

Captain Jefferson Davis "Oz" Carson sat in the pilot's seat of the black aircraft. His muscled, masculine features and blue eyes were hidden by an olive-green helmet and Nomax suit. The sun visor of his helmet was lowered to filter out the bright spring sunlight streaming through the windscreen of the chopper.

"Loop time," the pilot told his air crew. The even tone of his Virginia drawl belied the tension he felt, anticipating the difficult maneuver.

The MH-60K he controlled was incapable of executing a complete loop. But as the most skilled pilot in the U.S. Army, Oz was going to take the helicopter as close to a loop as was aerodynamically possible in the chopper. And while he had performed

5

the stunt many times before, he'd never done it before a huge audience.

The pilot continued to raise the collective pitch lever in his gloved left hand while flexing the control column forward with his right to bank the aircraft away from the grandstands. With an angry whopping, the pitch of the four main blades increased for maximum speed.

Oz lifted the MH-60K into a giddy tail-down position; the G-force of the steep climb squashed the crew into their seats. The chopper cut through the top of its near loop and—just as suddenly—the crew was almost weightless as the MH-60K nosed around and dropped.

Oz let out his breath, the tension vanishing from his muscles as the maneuver was completed. The rest of the exercise will be a piece of cake, he told himself. "Ready with the rockets?" Oz asked. He straightened the chopper so it rushed downward toward the airstrip that was now far below and ahead of them.

"Armed and ready," Lieutenant Chad "Death Song" Norton answered. Sitting in the gunner/navigator seat to the right of Oz, the rail-thin co-pilot had the virtual image display—VID—extended so it was practically in his lap. The high-resolution "TV" sight was linked to a chin-mounted FLIR; the screen showed the target area for the two TOW missiles mounted on the helicopter's modified ETS-style pylon.

"Death Song, I'll launch three rockets," Oz told his co-pilot as they hurtled toward the airstrip.

"Then you hit the APC on the field with a TOW. You'll have to be quick or we'll overshoot the target.

"O.T.," the pilot addressed his warrant officer, who sat behind Oz in the gunners' compartment, "you'll fire your Minigun at the APC after the TOW is launched."

"Got it," O.T.'s voice crackled on the intercom.

"Luger, you fire when we circle the target," Oz ordered. For a moment the pilot thought the control column of the chopper had failed to respond, but then decided it had just been his imagination.

"That's a roger," Luger answered.

"And remember to hold your fire any time your Miniguns are even slightly aimed in the direction of the grandstand," Oz cautioned his men, although all were aware of the extra care that had to exercised, even with the blanks and unarmed rockets they would be firing.

"Damn," Oz swore under his breath.

Death Song glanced at the pilot.

"Control column seems to be getting sluggish," Oz explained. "It's okay now. We'll continue our run."

Their target was now within range.

Oz tapped the launch button on the control column with the little finger of his right hand. Three folding-fin, 2.75-inch rockets packed in the 12-rocket pod to his right hissed to life, jumping from their tubes. They streamed on tails of fire toward the French-made AMX-10 Armored Personnel Carrier on the ground ahead of them. The rockets left a dim trail of smoke that the MH-60K whipped through as it charged after them toward the tank-like APC.

"Launching TOW," Death Song announced.

The missile thundered from its tube and arched to the APC ahead of the American chopper. Death Song held the two joysticks attached to the virtual image display, carefully guiding the rocket to its target, while Oz held the helicopter dead on course.

A wire unspooled behind the rocket; it carried the electronic impulses from the helicopter to the TOW, directing it to the target. Within a fraction of a second, the missile collided with the nose of the tank-like APC and bounced off the armored vehicle without damaging it.

O.T.'s Minigun commenced firing from the helicopter's side door. Oz took the helicopter to the right of the APC; O.T.'s motorized weapon made a high-pitched crackling as its six barrels blazed.

The MH-60K whisked past the armored vehicle. Then Oz brought his chopper into a tight turn that took them around the target parked on the field below.

Although Oz knew the TOW had a dummy warhead, it was still somewhat of a surprise to him to go through the tight attack they'd completed without seeing the smoke and explosion that would normally ensue when a TOW connected with its target. He pushed the thought from his mind and concentrated on the mock battle they were waging.

O.T. quit firing after they rounded the AMX-10. Oz twirled the chopper around and banked again, keeping the APC inside a tight circle that nearly set the MH-60K on its side. "Disarm our rockets," he ordered Death Song. "Damn this control column!"

"Rockets disarmed," Death Song reported. "Want me to take over?"

"Yeah, something's wrong with my stick," Oz replied.

They switched over and the helicopter went out of control. "Take it back!" Death Song yelled into the intercom. "I've got nothing at all here!"

The helicopter jumped into a tight circle, the ground rushing toward the nose of the aircraft.

Oz kicked a pedal to reduce their circular motion as he yanked on the cyclic pitch lever to lift them into the air.

"Close," Oz said half to himself. "Luger, go ahead and empty your gun at the tank. Let's get this over with and take this chopper back to the hangar."

"Yes, sir," the shaken gunner said. The blasts from Luger's Minigun, mounted in the gunner's door behind Oz, ripped the warm Paris air as the pilot completed the circuit of the APC, nearly skimming the tarmac.

Oz came out of the turn and spoke on the intercom, "Cease fire." He brought the helicopter up and kicked his right pedal to face the grandstand. "O.T. and Luger, disconnect your weapons. We can't afford any mistakes with this many people around. The controls seem all right again, but you'd better hang on. I'm going to take us back—"

Without warning the chopper accelerated toward the stands.

Oz pulled on the control column as the helicopter hurtled toward the crowd in the bleachers. Failing to slow the machine, he kicked the right rudder pedal, causing the helicopter to flip in a complete circuit as it continued toward the stands.

The crowd thought they were witnessing a well-rehearsed stunt. Applause rose from the crowd as Oz fought to regain control of the MH-60K.

Nearing the front of the grandstand, the controls finally responded as the chopper grazed the tarmac. Oz lifted it back into the air and brought its forward motion to a halt. It hung motionless in the air, just meters from the front row of onlookers.

The throng in the stands continued to applaud.

Oz backed the helicopter a safe distance from them and then dipped the chin of the helicopter into a mechanical bow that was recognizable as such to the crowd.

His feat brought a swell of applause.

Oz kicked a pedal to face the chopper toward the right, pushed the control column hard forward, and sped off the airstrip toward the hangar.

Just minutes after Oz had landed the MH-60K, he was relating his disturbing story to the members of his ground crew. The puzzled mechanics wheeled the helicopter into the hangar and started their inspection.

O.T. and Oz slowly and silently walked out of the hangar. Oz's hands still shook from the adrenaline coursing through his bloodstream. Taking a deep breath of warm air, he tried to calm himself. He removed his helmet and felt a craving for a cigarette.

"Well done," a thickly accented Russian voice declared from behind the pilot.

The two Americans turned to face the speaker, a short, robust man dressed in a brown jumpsuit. The Soviet uniform was easily recognizable with its transparent panel in the left front leg of the suit.

"Major Peter Komonsky of Voyenno Vozdushnize Sily," the man introduced himself, nervously extending his hand.

Oz hesitated only a fraction of a second before shaking the Soviet Air Force Major's hand. "Captain Carson," the pilot responded. "And this is Warrant Officer Harvey Litwin."

"Pleasure to meet," Komonsky said, shaking O.T.'s meaty paw. "This is my gunner, Captain Alexei Nitschke."

Nitschke stepped forward and nodded. The Soviet gunner's handsome dark hair and skin revealed his Mongolian heritage. Oz had heard that the Soviet system resisted the advancement of non-Russian troops so he naturally assumed that the Mongolian must possess extraordinary flying skills to have become a captain in the Soviet Air Force.

"We operate new Mi-35 in air show," Nitschke explained to Oz. "The one your American military calls 'Hind-K.' "

"Ah," Oz nodded. He wondered for a moment if the Soviets had had anything to do with the near disaster of the MH-60K, but pushed the thought out of his mind. "I'm looking forward to seeing you fly. You're scheduled for tomorrow?"

"Da," Nitschke nodded.

"Oz?" Komonsky asked, reading the name painted on the helmet tucked under the American pilot's arm.

A flicker of a smile danced across Oz's face. "That's my handle."

Noting the Soviet's look of puzzlement, O.T. added, "His nickname. Nom de guerre."

Nitschke smiled and nodded in recognition. He turned toward Komonsky and spoke rapidly in his native tongue. After a moment, Nitschke turned back to the Americans. "You are Oz who fought our renegade troops in Antarctica? So, you must be elite Night Stalkers fliers in U.S. Army?"

"Well, I . . ." Oz hesitated.

"Ah, no can tell secrets," Komonsky nodded in understanding. "We in USSR understand need for secrets," he reassured Oz. "You do bang-up job flying today."

"Thanks," Oz said, again wondering if the Soviets were somehow connected to the near tragedy.

"Now we go to grandstand," Komonsky continued. "We want catch Superstealth show. Nice meeting you."

"Nice meeting you," Oz replied. "Good luck tomorrow."

The two Soviet airmen abruptly turned and left. As they walked away, Oz could hear his name mentioned several times in a storm of Russian.

"What was that all about?" Death Song asked as he approached Oz and O.T.

"Some of Oz's admirers," O.T. chuckled. "Captain, it's lucky we're enjoying another period of *glasnost.* If even the *Soviet* chopper pilots know you by name, there'd be a price on your head for sure!"

"I guess that's comforting," Oz responded. "I have a feeling those guys weren't your run-of-the-mill Soviet pilots, though. I'm betting they're our Russian counterparts if they're flying the Hind-K in tomorrow's demonstrations."

"Yeah," Death Song agreed, "you can bet the Soviets aren't going to let just anyone fly their newest battle wagon."

"Well, I think I'm still going to go up and see the Superstealth," Oz said. "There's nothing we can do around here." He turned and yelled toward the hangar, "Hey, Luger, you want to go and see the show with us?"

"Yes, sir," Luger called, jogging the short distance from the hangar.

Sergeant Bruce Marvin, the helicopter's ground crew chief, walked out of the hangar and approached the four fliers. The man had a neckless bulldog head connected to his barrel chest. His arms and shoulders were well muscled from over a decade of repairing, disassembling, and reassembling Army helicopters.

"We still haven't discovered what's fouled up, Captain," the Sergeant said when he reached Oz. "But my monkeys'll tear her down to its bolts if we need to. We'll find out what went wrong and get it right. With any luck, we'll have your chariot ready for this afternoon's show."

The Paris Air Show dated back to 1909 when it was first held as the *L'Esposition de la Locomotion Aerienne.* Since then, it had gradually grown to become a matter of international prestige to the companies and nations displaying aircraft and equipment at the aerospace exhibition. This year, the show was held at the Le Bourget Airport northeast of Paris proper, just outside the city's "department boundary."

The United States had a national pavilion with over one hundred firms represented, with everything from jet aircraft to the newest guided missiles designed for air-to-air combat. NASA had a mock-up of the manned spaceship Congress had authorized for a round trip to Mars.

A biennial event, the air show had enjoyed good attendance this year with 700,000 visitors expected before the show closed on the eighth of June, after an eleven-day run. Throughout the exhibition, aircraft in developmental stages were displayed in the form of models; planes in production took part in the hundreds of in-flight demonstrations like the one Oz and his men had given. These allowed aircraft to be shown at their best to potential international buyers.

There was increased competition among the exhibitors for Third-world and anti-terrorist sales due to yet another year of renewed peace gestures between the USSR and the West. Adding to the intense bids for dwindling military sales was the entry of Soviet and other former Eastern-bloc countries into the arms arena with low-budget fighter jets.

For the competition, the American, British, French, and Soviet military planes were flown by military personnel who were familiar with the equipment and could milk the last bit of performance from the aircraft. The flight demonstrations of the last few days had been spectacular.

Soon, Oz and his crew were jostling their way to four empty seats they had spied in the thronging grandstand. The spring sunlight bathed the bleachers in its warmth, but a bank of dark clouds in the west rumbled ominously with distant thunder.

As the American helicopter crew climbed the steep steps leading to the empty seats, it seemed to Oz that the whole crowd was tensed, waiting for the appearance of the Superstealth.

There was little doubt in Oz's mind that the hi-tech aircraft would be the show stopper of the entire exhibition. The new American fighter/bomber was officially named the XA-2011; but it had been dubbed the "Superstealth" by an aviation magazine because of the rumors of its capabilities. The name had stuck and was now even used by the plane's manufacturer.

The jet had been created as a competitor to the European Fighter/Attack Aircraft developed by the Eurofighter consortium consisting of British, West German, Italian, and Spanish companies. But the Superstealth had become more than a competitor; it now overshadowed the EF/AA because of the capabilities it was rumored to possess.

"The big question," Death Song said over the murmuring of the crowd as the Americans inched along the row toward their seats, "is *if* the plane can do everything it's supposed to be able to do."

"There's no way it can do everything," O.T. answered as he squeezed past a man puffing at a cigarette holder. "I'm betting the advanced leaks and publicity the Superstealth's got are going to hurt it. Stuff like saying it can fly silently and is nearly invisible is going to make everyone disappointed when it finally makes its appearance."

"I don't know," Luger said, settling his wiry frame into a seat beside Oz. "It really might be possible to mount miniature cameras surrounded by LCD color TV screens plastering a plane's skin. If they piped the pictures to the screen on the other side of the plane, it'd be almost like seeing right through the plane. It'd look invisible from a distance."

"I'll believe it when I see it," O.T. responded, shaking his clean-shaven head in disbelief. "Of course I guess we know that nearly silent flight is possible," he added in a low voice.

The others said nothing. They knew it was possible to cancel nearly all the noise of an aircraft since they occasionally used such a device on their own MH-60K. The mechanism employed a huge speaker array that created a negative counterpart to the helicopter's engine and blade noise. The result was an effective cancellation of much of the MH-60K engine and rotor noise. But making the louder engines of a jet plane silent and the plane invisible, too, was a different proposition that would require a distinct increase in capabilities over any previous stealth aircraft that were invisible to radar only.

Before any of the Night Stalkers could say anything more, a loud murmuring rippled through the audience. Oz turned to see what was happening as agitated voices were raised throughout the crowd.

People were pointing at the field. The pilot stared in the direction they pointed, now aware of a low whishing sound that had gone unnoticed.

A ghostly shadow of an aircraft floated across the field. The source of the shadow and whishing sound was nowhere to be seen.

"Will you look at that!" Luger exclaimed. The shadow inched closer to the grandstand as everyone in the audience stared at it.

"Ladies and Gentlemen," the announcer's French-accented voice boomed from the public address loudspeakers, "the XA-2011 Superstealth."

The Night Stalkers stood in wonder with the rest of the crowd. The plane wasn't totally invisible. Oz could make out a shimmering, mirage-like spot that could barely be seen hovering over the shadow on the tarmac. As it came closer, he could see dust being kicked by a whirlwind of invisible activity.

"Damn," O.T. muttered. "It's almost on top of the stands and we didn't even notice it. Unless you know right where to look, you'd miss it."

There was a twinkling in the air in front of the stands, then suddenly the fighter bomber seemed to materialize. It hung nearly motionless like a Harrier, its engines vented downward to balance it on jets of hot gases. The jet's engines screamed with a high-pitched whine accompanied by a blast of hot air. Those around Oz covered their ears as the intense sound engulfed them.

Then the noise dropped to a low rumble as the cancellation circuit inside the plane was again activated. A Superstealth crewman threw a second bank of switches and the aircraft flickered and became transparent with the energizing of the cloaking system.

The crowd was silent for a moment. Then a wave of applause, shouting, and nervous laughter engulfed the audience, delighted by the wonder they had witnessed.

Oz pulled off his mirrored Gargoyles sunglasses and stared at the position the plane had occupied. Only the slight shimmering pattern and the shadow on the tarmac below the bomber divulged the presence of the jet even at its close proximity to the grandstand. As Oz watched, the mirage in the air rose on nearly silent blasts from its jets. The air seemed to glisten as the bomber swung about and rapidly accelerated with a loud hissing.

The announcer's voice continued from the loudspeakers, "The Osbourn-Norton XA-2011 Superstealth has—as you can *not* see—a wide range of electronic countermeasures capable of making it invisible to both the naked eye and radar. This hi-tech plane is capable of carrying a weapon load of 68,000 kilograms to a distance of 4,850 kilometers without refueling."

The shimmering raced across the field as the plane climbed, gaining speed and altitude. Oz lost sight of the quivering distortion that marked the plane's position as the announcer's voice continued, "Weapons include air-to-air and air-to-surface missiles, a trainable 30mm cannon, and all types of standard bombs associated with this type of aircraft."

"Like nukes," O.T. said under his breath.

"In addition to a weapons control officer and pilot," the announcer continued, "the plane has a third crew member assigned to electronic countermeasures.

"In order to power the electrical needs of the Superstealth, the aircraft carries an on-board nuclear reactor similar to those used by many countries in their space programs. The unit is armored to prevent accidental spills during a crash or other accident, though the reactor's geometric shielding—its distance from the crew—must be augmented by a portable lead and steel shield added by the ground crew after the Superstealth lands.

"Now," the announcer continued, "if you'll direct your attention to the far end of the field . . ."

Oz squinted in the sunlight, looking to the position the announcer had suggested. The Superstealth winked into existence as its cloak was shut off; an instant later, its jets thundered when the noise cancellation was curtailed. The pilot took the plane above the grandstands, the Superstealth's engines roaring and shaking the earth.

"For more information about the XA-2011 Superstealth," the announcer resumed his speech, "be sure to check Osbourn-Norton representatives in the United States Pavilion. We think you'll—"

"Well, let's go find some crow for me to eat," O.T. joked to his fellow crew members still standing around him. "I'd say they more than succeeded in creating an invisible bomber."

"Maybe we can get a closer look at the plane back at the hangars," Death Song suggested. "It's berthed right beside our MH-60K."

"Worth a try," Oz agreed as he stood with the others and inched his way back to the aisle. "But I doubt we can get too close," he continued. "Osbourn-Norton has been increasing its security over the last few weeks since they announced the arrest of a spy in their London plant."

*　　*　　*

A loud thunderclap announced the close proximity of the storm clouds that were nearing the airfield as the four Night Stalkers reached the Osbourn-Norton hangar. They watched as the Superstealth was carefully wheeled into the massive building.

The silver-gray skin of the plane was mottled by the densely-packed miniature cameras and LCD screens coating it. The twin-engined plane seemed larger up close even though its wingspan of 8.5 meters was small by bomber standards of several decades before. The ground crew carefully led the plane into its hangar, watching nervously to be sure the nuclear shielding assembly stayed put on the reactor in the tail of the Superstealth.

A guard, who wore a blue security uniform and carried an Enfield SA 80 slung on his shoulder, eyed the Night Stalkers carefully as the plane entered the hangar. The man's eyes shifted to three men in business suits standing in the distance. A second guard stood inside the hangar, nervously fingering the safety of his SA 80.

The recent rash of Euskadi ta Askatasuna terrorist attacks in Spain has made everyone extra cautious, Oz thought to himself. The terrorist attacks had also dictated that the four Night Stalkers wear pistols; French authorities had requested that military personnel visiting the Paris Air Show wear sidearms if they were trained to use them. Consequently, Oz had his Ruger P-85 holstered at his hip and the other members of his team also carried pistols.

Oz gave the guard a half salute as the man again glanced at the four Night Stalkers as the large hangar door the Superstealth had entered closed behind it.

The guard nodded toward the Americans as he backed into the small side door of the hangar. Once inside, he carefully closed and locked it.

"Well, that settles that," O.T. said.

"At least we got a closer look," Luger said. "It doesn't look too extraordinary without its circuits activated."

"Well, I'm going to get something to eat," Death Song said, fighting a yawn.

"Sounds like a good idea," O.T. nodded, eyeing the dark cloud that blotted out the sun. "Maybe we could—"

"Shhh," Oz hissed, a finger to his lips. "Listen!"

The four Americans were silent. A muffled thumping was barely discernible under the noise of distant jets landing at the nearby Charles de Gaulle Airport northeast of them.

"Silenced shots!" O.T. said.

"The guards?" Luger asked.

"No, they weren't carrying silenced weapons," Death Song replied.

"Come on," Oz ordered as he drew his pistol. He and his men broke into a run toward the Osbourn-Norton hangar where the gunshots had originated.

2

Oz raced to the hangar, jacking back his Ruger P-5's slide. He let the slide go; the action clattered forward, stripping a cartridge from the magazine and chambering it. The other three crew members did the same, their pistols clanking as they sprinted to the hangar.

As the four neared the building, Oz motioned with his finger toward the door. "We'll have to break it down."

"I've got it," O.T. volunteered. He jumped at the door with surprising speed considering his burly build. He slammed his booted foot against it, his full weight backing up the kick. The heavy door buckled in its frame and whipped open with a rending of metal and wood.

Oz dived through the open door to confront a man in gray overalls who stood with a dead guard at his feet. The man in overalls whirled around, raising the silenced Sterling submachine gun in his hands.

Before the killer could aim, Oz grabbed the barrel of the Sterling in his free hand, jerking it to one side. The American pilot gun-whipped the man across the temple, bowling him over.

Oz charged into the hangar, his men close behind. A furious humming of silenced bullets cut through the air around the Night Stalkers as they entered. Instinctively, the four Americans tumbled to the hard floor and dived behind the only cover there was in the nearly empty hangar—a row of drums filled with oil.

There was another long coughing of a silenced submachine gun. The bullets from another Sterling ricocheted off the floor and whined through the air next to them. A second burst thumped into the steel barrels, poking holes in their surfaces. Oil spurted onto the floor from the new holes.

In the moment it had taken to overpower the man at the door and dive through the doorway, Oz had seen the bodies of the ground crew and the other guard lying on the floor in pools of blood.

Oz turned to his men. "Ready?" he whispered to his men who were now sprawled behind the drums.

"Ready," O.T. said in a low voice, his Colt Double Eagle automatic held at the ready. The others nodded.

"Now!" Oz ordered his men.

With practiced precision, Oz and O.T. rose to a crouch. Simultaneously, Death Song and Luger rolled onto their stomachs to fire from prone positions on either side of the barrels.

Oz aimed his P-85 by reflex at one of the three armed men standing on the nearly empty floor in front of the Superstealth. He fired twice, catching his target in the chest. The man remained standing and jerked on the trigger of his silenced submachine gun.

The Americans dropped back behind the metal drums as the assailants answered their shots with a furious hail of gunfire. The bullets thumped through the heavy metal wall near Oz's men and cut more holes into the steel barrels.

There was a silence broken only by the sound of oil bleeding from the drums and the clatter of an empty Sterling magazine being dropped onto the concrete floor.

Oz peered around the barrel as the shooting stopped, loosing another volley at the man he had hit earlier. O.T., Death Song, and Luger launched another salvo at the men standing in the center of the hangar.

The target showed no reaction as Oz's bullets connected. Instead, he stood reloading his empty submachine gun.

"I'd swear I hit one of those guys twice!" O.T. yelled as he dropped back down, releasing the empty magazine from his Colt pistol and expertly shoving a loaded magazine home in its grip.

Another angry volley of shots bounced off the floor next to the Night Stalkers.

"They have ballistic vests!" Oz shouted to his companions above the din of the bullets striking the barrels. "Head shots. Now!"

The four Night Stalkers rose. They ignored the squall of shooting in front of them and took careful aim, pulled their triggers, and then dropped back to the comparative safety afforded by the barrels.

All was quiet.

Oz glanced around the barrels. The three lay sprawled on the floor, blood running from the head wounds they had sustained.

Without warning, a deafening hail of bullets came from the rear of the hangar to crash into the wall behind the Americans. The crack of the supersonic bullets was accompanied by the muzzle blast of an unsilenced SA-80 rifle. The din filled the building. Unlike the slower-moving submachine bullets, the rifle's projectiles cut through the barrels, narrowly missing the Americans and splashing them with oil and metal fragments.

O.T. sword loudly as he plastered himself against the floor to avoid the second salvo from the automatic rifle. The shooting ceased and the hangar was silent for several seconds.

"Now what?" Luger asked.

Oz rose on his elbows and studied the bullet holes in the wall. He made a quick calculation as to the path the bullets had taken to reach them. "He must be at the back of the hangar, near the Super-stealth's tail," the pilot whispered in the tomb-like silence. He quickly glanced around the corner of the barrel, fired three rapid shots, and then pulled his head back behind the cover.

There was another string of automatic rifle fire near where Oz's head had been.

Then the shooting ceased.

"I can't see anything back there," Oz whispered, dropping the half expended magazine from his P-85 and inserting a fresh one. "It's too dark in there to see whoever's shooting. Let's sit tight and keep them bottled up here in the hangar."

"Yeah," O.T. said. "The frogs guarding the air show will have the firepower we need."

"Someone must have heard all the shooting," Death Song agreed.

"Right," Oz said. "We have whoever's in here cut off from the exits. Time's on our side; let's sit tight and wait."

The clouds made the interior of the hangar even darker.

All was again deathly still.

Then there was a loud roll of thunder outside and, as if answering the sound, the motors on the hangar doors were activated. As the large doors cracked open, first one and then both jet engines of the Superstealth started a soft whining that quickly built to a roar.

C H A P T E R

3

Thank God they've engaged the noise cancellation circuit on the Superstealth, Oz thought. Otherwise, everyone inside the metal hangar would have been deafened. But the fumes and back blast from the jet's exhaust were nearly overwhelming as the plane's engines strained to push the aircraft out of the hangar.

Coughing, Oz cautiously rose to his right knee. He glared into the back of the dark hangar. A flash of lightning from the direction of the open hangar door illuminated the Superstealth and the back of the hangar for just an instant. Oz could discern the dark form of the rifleman who had the Americans pinned behind the drums.

The pilot held his P-85 tightly in both hands as he aimed at the shadowed corner where the man was hidden. The American fired a long string of shots into the darkness at the half-hidden man, pumping the trigger rapidly to quickly empty his pistol.

Oz dropped to his knees. Since he had exhausted the ammunition he'd been carrying, he thumbed the slide release on the side of the P-85 and reholstered the pistol. "Stay down," he shouted to his men.

The jet was now nearly out of the hangar, but the back blast from its engines stung Oz's eyes as he glanced at it. Shielding his face with his hand, he cautiously peered around the drum toward the darkness at the back of the hangar.

Oz waited for another flash of lightning—or a rifle shot. He clenched his teeth, hoping it wouldn't be the latter and momentarily wondered if he was silhouetted in front of the doorway behind him.

Another flash revealed the prone form of the rifleman Oz had fired at. Oz turned to his men, thunder rumbling in the distance. "It's clear," he yelled as he rose to his feet. "Come on."

The Night Stalkers jumped to their feet and ran toward the hangar door, pursuing the Superstealth, which was nearly out of the hangar. The exhaust of the jets was vented downward slightly as the plane's pilot prepared to lift the aircraft into the air.

Oz scooped up one of the SA-80 rifles that lay on the floor near the hangar doorway and whirled around, inspecting the inside of the hangar once more to be sure no one was hiding. Seeing no one, he turned back to the hangar door and raced through it to stand by his men.

The Superstealth quietly lifted into the air, hovered a moment, then started a fast ascent straight up into the blackness brought about by the heavy cloud cover. Huge drops of rain splattered the runway and threatened to soak Oz and his men.

"What are they doing?" Luger asked as they stood watching the aircraft float into the storm.

"I'm not sure," Oz yelled over the wind that was starting to whip the rain into their faces. "They're probably taking the plane to safety—they couldn't be sure who was winning the gun battle in the hangar."

"Yeah," O.T. agreed. "That plane's their number one priority. Protecting it was all they were concerned about."

"Come on," Oz said. "Let's get to our chopper and see if we can reach them on the radio."

"Wait!" O.T. yelled as they turned to leave. "There're activating the visual stealth circuits."

"What?" Oz demanded, turning back to face the rising aircraft. Sure enough, the machine had nearly vanished. Only its tail section, apparently damaged by the gunfire, remained visible in the storm raging around it.

"Why'd they do that?" Luger asked.

"There's only one reason for the men on that jet to activate its stealth features," Oz said. "They're intent on escaping from the airfield without being caught. Let's contact the authorities."

Running back to the American hangar, the four Night Stalkers found Sergeant Marvin standing in the rain.

"What's all the shooting about?" the Sergeant asked, following them into the hangar.

"Somebody's stolen the Superstealth," Oz answered.

Marvin swore. "Your chopper's repaired if that's any—"

"Ready to fly?" Oz asked.

"Some kind of gadget was inserted into your controls. We removed it and just refueled your chopper."

Within minutes, the ground crew had the helicopter pushed out into the rain.

"You still see it, O.T.?" Oz asked as he raised the collective pitch lever in his left hand, lifting the helicopter into the air. The warrant officer had stayed outside in the rain watching the Superstealth. Now he gazed through the open gunner's door, using a pair of binoculars he kept in the helicopter to search the storm.

"Negative, Captain," O.T. replied on the intercom as he wiped the mist off the lenses of the binoculars. "But they turned and headed northeast—at about 45 degrees from true north, as nearly as I can reckon the direction in this storm. They maintained that heading until I lost 'em."

"Their tail remained visible?" Oz asked.

"Right. They're moving quite slowly and not impossible to spot. But this heavy rain has started to limit visibility."

"Here's the map of the area," Death Song told Oz as he punched up a topographical map on one of the two cathode ray tube displays in front of the pilot. The instruments in the cabin glowed an eerie green in the near darkness of the storm. A gust of wind splattered rain onto the side of the black MH-60K helicopter.

Oz watched the CRT as he pushed his right pedal, rotating the helicopter's nose to put them onto course; the wind buffeted the chopper and splattered the windscreen with rain that was quickly sloshed off by the dual windshield wipers. Lightning flashed in the black mantle of clouds above them, bleaching the airport below.

Studying the sky ahead of him, Oz brought the chopper to its top speed. "We're going to have to stay sharp. It'd be easy to run over them, as hard as they are to see, if they're still traveling at a slow speed. Holler out if you see anything."

Oz selected the international emergency frequency of 121.5 megacycles and toggled on his radio. "This is aircraft MH-60K NS-1 calling Charles de Gaulle Airport. Please acknowledge, over."

The lightning made a crackle in his headphones, then an accented voice spoke in English, the language normally used at international airports. "This is air traffic control at Charles de Gaulle. We read you loud and clear NS-1. Is this an emergency? Over."

"Roger, Charles de Gaulle," Oz replied. "And please patch our conversation through to your military frequencies, if possible. In addition to our helicopter, we believe you have an unidentified aircraft—a Superstealth—that will be, or already is, in your air space. The plane has been stolen from a hangar at Le Bourget Airport; we are in pursuit of it. The Superstealth will not, I repeat, will *not* appear on your radar. I believe it will cross the northern corner of your field. We are approximately 5 kilometers southwest of you. Over."

"NG-1, is this some kind of joke? We have no report of any stolen plane, and you are on the frequency normally reserved for emergencies. Stiff penalties can be levied if you persist in this prank. Please sign off immediately. Over."

The exasperation showed in Oz's voice as he spoke, "This is not a joke. Get us patched through to your military and clear the northern approach to your airfield or you will be risking innocent lives. The plane ahead of us is very hard to detect and is equipped with a stealth surface so it will not appear on your radar. Over."

There was a brief pause and then Oz's radio crackled to life as the air traffic controller finally responded. "All right, NS-1. We've just received word that the XA-2011 Superstealth has been stolen. We are diverting all traffic on the northern approaches to our field right now. Please keep us advised of your position. We will keep this channel open. We're now relaying your message to our Air Force. Over."

"Thanks Charles de Gaulle, we will keep you advised, over and out."

"At two o'clock," Death Song said over the intercom.

Oz squinted into the night-like darkness caused by the thick cloud cover. After a second, he spotted the tail of the aircraft. It seemed to be floating by itself, the plane it belonged to being totally invisible in the rain. "No mistaking this one," Oz said. "That's got to be it."

He triggered the switch on his control column and again spoke over the radio. "Charles de Gaulle, this is NS-1. The Superstealth is definitely headed your way. We will follow it, assuming its altitude and flight path. We are coming in low and may be obscured by ground clutter.'' He checked the vertical situation display, which listed all aspects of the MH-60K's flight path including its radar altitude. "We are at 500 meters and about a kilometer behind the Superstealth. Over."

"We have one plane on our scope, NS-1," the radio replied. "We're assuming that the blip is you and the Superstealth is directly ahead of you. The French Air Force is scrambling five Rafale jets to help you. But their ETA will be at least ten minutes. The fliers want to know how you're tracking the Superstealth. Over."

"The cloaking on the plane's tail isn't functioning," Oz replied. "Possibly the nose is visible as well. But tell the fighter pilots to approach it with caution or they'll be eating its exhaust fumes before they see it. Over."

"I'll relay your warning. Good luck, NS-1."

"Thanks Charles de Gaulle. Over and out."

"Ten minutes before the Rafales get here," Death Song said in disbelief. "They must be walking."

"Let's just sit tight," Oz said. "The Superstealth have any radar on us?"

"I've been watching," Death Song answered. "Right now all I have are the scans from Charles de Gaulle and Le Bourget. But I'm pretty sure they scanned us a moment ago. There it is again. I'm pretty sure they've swept us."

"Better hang on everyone," Oz warned his crew. "They'll probably take evasive maneuvers shortly."

They continued on for several minutes before

the Superstealth finally made its move. The nearly invisible plane veered off its course, dropping slightly to gain speed and banking hard to its left. The tail section winked, vanishing for a few seconds and then reappearing.

"We're circling to the north, possibly back toward central Paris," Oz warned Charles de Gaulle over the radio as he kicked the left pedal to turn the chopper into its new course heading behind the Superstealth. "The plane became totally invisible for a few seconds but the tail is now visible again. Over."

"We copy."

"Captain, better take us down to match their altitude," Death Song suggested.

"Good idea," Oz agreed. "That'll let the French get some idea of the Superstealth's altitude." The MH-60K responded smoothly as Oz depressed the collective pitch lever leveling with the jet ahead of them. The helicopter dropped and lurched with a cross wind that brought a brief shower of rain splattering against the side of the chopper.

Oz studied the horizontal situation display. Connected to the chopper's mission control computer, the display showed a map that was generated from a data cartridge of the navigation points in the area around Paris. This map was coupled with a reading they had taken earlier from the U.S. Satellite Global Positioning System. The computer and positioning reference made it possible to find their exact position within a few feet as they traveled over the French countryside rushing below them.

The pilot triggered his radio again, "This is

NS-1. We are directly above Aubervillers and are continuing toward central Paris. Over."

"NS-1, we are still barely tracking you above the ground clutter," a new voice answered. Oz assumed a supervisor had stepped into the radio loop once the seriousness of the emergency was recognized. "ETA for the Rafales is five minutes. Over."

Oz booted his left rudder pedal slightly and nudged the control column to the left to counteract the buffeting wind that strained to shove them off course. "What I don't understand," the pilot said over the intercom, "is why they aren't flying at maximum speed. If they kicked it, they could lose us in a couple of minutes."

"Maybe their engines were damaged in the gunfight," O.T. suggested.

"Well, whatever it is," Oz said, "I'm just glad that—"

"It's winked off again!" Death Song warned Oz as the tail section of the Superstealth ahead of them again vanished.

"We'll stay on this heading and hope they reappear," Oz said evenly. "Anyone see anything?"

"There they are," Luger yelled. "At one o'clock."

"I've got them." Oz adjusted their course so they were again tailing the Superstealth.

"Tried to sneak out on us," Death Song chided.

"And almost succeeded," Oz added, glancing downward at the city of Paris as it was lit by a flash of lightning. The buildings flashing below them appeared to be crisscrossed by a haphazard network of canals. Only the cars and buses showed that the dark, wet stretches were really water-choked streets rather than waterways.

"We're over the Place de la Concorde," Oz radioed as his chopper hurtled over the open courtyard below. The area was easily recognized from the air by its distinctive fountains and Egyptian obelisk. "We're continuing across the Seine and appear to be headed for the Champ de Mars. Over."

"Vanished again," Death Song warned. "Looked like he was going to round the Eiffel Tower."

"I agree," Oz said. "But I'm slowing just in case. It would be easy to run into him in this weather. He wasn't traveling too fast and he might try to hover so we'll overshoot him."

"Yeah," Death Song agreed. "Anyone who's crazy enough to overfly an airport might chance that."

Oz slowed as they approached the open steel skeleton of the Eiffel Tower. The monument stood on its four feet, its spire silhouetted in the light reflected from the Seine river looping to the west of the structure.

"There it is," O.T. yelled over the intercom. "At nine o'clock."

Oz wheeled the helicopter into a tight turn that took them toward the Superstealth. The gray aircraft was totally visible in the downpour of rain. The jet hovered over the Seine, facing the helicopter as the Americans rounded the Eiffel Tower.

"Looks like they're waiting for us," Death Song said.

Oz pulled back on the control column to slow

his chopper's speed. "Either the cloaking has completely failed or they've shut it down."

"They couldn't be armed, could they?" O.T. asked.

"Good question," Oz answered as he brought the helicopter to a standstill so they hung immobile, facing the Superstealth.

The two aircraft hung in the air over the city. Gusts buffeted the planes with sheets of water. "Superstealth," Oz called. "Can you read me? Over." There was no answer. He tried several other frequencies and then discontinued the effort to contact the plane.

The radio crackled in Oz's headset. "NS-1, this is French Air Force RA-25, can you read us? Over."

Oz engaged the trigger-like radio switch on his control column. "Roger, RA-25. This is NS-1."

"We've got your chopper on our scopes. We'll be on top of you in 60 seconds. Where's the SS you've been tagging? Over."

"The Superstealth is to the west of us hanging in place above the Seine. It's currently stationary with no movement. Over."

"We'll get it. Sit tight while we force it to land. All right, I have a visual on it. Over."

At that instant, the Superstealth started to wheel around, vanishing as it accelerated.

"NS-1! Where did the Superstealth go?" the French pilot called. His white and red jet streaked past Oz, its wake rocking the MH-60K. There was a flurry of swearing in French, and then the radio was clear for Oz to answer.

"You just missed hitting him," Oz warned.

"You should be able to just barely see him. He's heading north."

"Where? I see nothing." The jet pulled through a tight turn and darted downward again.

"Look out!" Oz warned over the radio. "You'll ram him if you're not careful! Pull up. Pull up now!"

The jet fighter leaped skyward, narrowly missing the shimmering mirage that marked the Superstealth's position.

"RA-25," Oz spoke into the radio, "the aircraft makes only a glittering distortion in the air. It appears transparent. Bring your jet to its lowest cruising speed and keep your eyes peeled. Over."

"Still can't see a thing," the Rafale pilot yelled over the radio as he circled and dropped his altitude once more.

"We don't see it either," another of the jet pilots said over the radio. He began to speak in French and was answered a moment later by another radio caller.

Oz wished he could understand the exchange.

"I can't make it all out," Death Song said after listening to the conversation. "But I think RA-25 ordered his men to stay above us."

"That's a good idea," Oz said. "If they get a couple of more planes down here, someone's going to collide with the Superstealth. They don't know what they're looking for." He toggled on his radio, "RA-25, this is NS-1. Let us follow the Superstealth if you're having trouble locating him."

"Negative, NS-1, we can handle it. Sit tight and we'll take care of it from here."

There was the splattering of rain on the windscreen of the MH-60K and Oz lost sight of the shimmering pattern of the Superstealth that nearly melted into the gray Parisian skyline.

RA-25 shot by the Night Stalker's chopper once more. The French plane was headed south.

A gust rocked the chopper and, when Oz compensated, abated unexpectedly, forcing Oz to sling the column over briskly to keep them in position. "RA-25," Oz radioed as he regained sight of the shimmering pattern once more, "I think the Superstealth is heading north. You are headed the wrong way. Over."

"North?" RA-25 asked. "Are you sure, NS-1? Over."

"I have a visual on him again. He's definitely headed north . . . Wait. I've lost my visual on him. Please let us head north, we might be able to locate him for you. Over."

"Negative, negative," RA-25 answered. "You Yanks sit tight and stay out of our way. Let us handle this—this is a French matter. We're switching to our military frequency. Over and out."

"They're going to lose it," Death Song said quietly as he watched the jet roll and race northward.

"Afraid so," Oz agreed, shaking his head. "We've lost it. The way it was angling off true north when we last saw it, it could be almost anywhere out there."

Oz triggered the radio again, "This is NS-1. Our weather is deteriorating. We request permission to head back to Le Bourget Airport. Over."

"This is Le Bourget, NS-1," a voice answered over the radio. "You have permission to head straight to the airport. Please stay below three hundred meters and approach directly from the southeast.''

"Are the Rafales having any luck in locating the Superstealth?''

"We have no report, but I think it's a negative, NS-1. We've been watching them on our radar and the planes are all over the place. I don't think they have a clue as to where the Superstealth is headed. Sorry for the bad news. Over."

"I imagine anyone would have lost it in this weather," Oz said, aware of the need not to hurt the pride of the Frenchmen involved in the search. Even so, he felt angry that the Rafale pilot had caused the Americans to lose their chance to trail the Superstealth. "Thanks for helping us," Oz added. "NS-1 over and out."

Oz studied his HSD and started a slow swing that took them around the Eiffel Tower. He set the MH-60K onto its new heading that glowed on the instrument display. "Okay, everyone," he said over the intercom, "we're returning to Le Bourget."

"We're on a collision course!" the weapons control engineer exclaimed.

Joseph Stakem, the pilot of the Superstealth, checked the display in front of him. "I see it," he said calmly over the plane's intercom. "Are you positive our cloaking circuits are working now?"

"All green," the electronic countermeasures engineer answered irritably.

Stakem wondered how the French fighter had managed to intercept them. The pilot watched the dot on the forward screen that had appeared inside the computer-generated radar image. The Superstealth's circuitry highlighted the approaching jet on the display, along with data identifying it as a French Rafale.

Stakem shoved forward on the control stick between his knees, the Superstealth diving so quickly the crew hung weightless in their shoulder harnesses. The ground raced toward them as he leveled out. He stared upward and was relieved to see that the French jet didn't counter his move.

"They're passing over us," the weapons control engineer said needlessly.

The pilot studied the screens around him and then checked his flight computer display. The storm was well behind them now and there were no planes of any kind nearby. He had finally eluded the last of the aircraft that had hounded them ever since the American chopper had spotted the Superstealth.

For all the good it does us, Stakem thought. The glowing fuel indicator was at zero; the Superstealth was out of fuel for all practical purposes. The pilot quietly cursed their luck. He decided to conserve their last precious gallons of fuel. "I'm putting us on autopilot, now that we're out of the storm's turbulence. Any good ideas where we should put down?"

No one answered him. Stakem relaxed for a moment and monitored the autopilot to be sure it was functioning correctly. The huge machine was so full of bugs, he found he didn't trust anything to really work properly. The computer lifted them upward slightly to clear a grove of trees, then quickly dropped them down again. Everything seemed all right.

The Superstealth traveled almost silently, a fact that Stakem couldn't get used to. Even worse, as far as the young pilot was concerned, was the lack of any accurate view of the outside world. Large screens lining the inside of the cockpit displayed images piped in from the tiny color cameras mounted on the skin of the Superstealth. Stakem felt as if he were riding in the middle of a giant video game.

"I think I've found a landing point on the STARS," Guy Volland, the weapons control engineer said. Since the plane was unarmed, Volland had been acting as the pilot's navigator. "Let me transfer it onto your HSD." He awkwardly punched the proper buttons along the unfamiliar cathode ray tube screen in front of him, transferring the image of the STARS—stored terrain and access retrieval system— to the pilot's monitor.

Stakem studied the STARS for a moment. The picture gave a three-dimensional view of the earth's surface ahead of them with an artificial sun-shading clearly showing the elevations. "Mark SB23?" the pilot asked, reading the co-ordinates of the closest reference point.

"Right," Volland replied. "That's one of the emergency landing spots we programmed into our STARS. It's almost dead ahead of us. An old farm with a large grain elevator."

Stakem didn't like the idea of trying to land in the open. Nothing had gone right so far and this looked like another snafu. He'd been told there would be no bloodshed when they stole the aircraft, but Hauschild and Volland—the two men riding with him now in the Superstealth—had gunned down the rest of the flight crew and the ground team as well.

Under French law, Stakem knew he was just as guilty of murder as the two who had pulled the triggers. There was no turning back now and he had no intention of getting caught if he could avoid it.

"Let's give the farm a try," the pilot said reluctantly. "If we can find somewhere to sit tight, maybe we can keep from being spotted until they can get some more fuel to us. Do we have enough juice left to make it?"

Volland checked his instruments and typed in some figures on the keyboard in front of him. "We should just make it. ETA in five minutes. Just stay on the course marked."

"Are the cloaking circuits still working?" Stakem asked his electronics countermeasures engineer, Jim Hauschild, who sat behind him and to his right. Stakem didn't trust the engineer's abilities. Hauschild had failed to note that the stealth circuits on the tail section were faulty, and that mistake had nearly gotten them forced down by the French fighter jets.

"Everything's operational," Hauschild replied, sounding tired. Then he sat up in his flight couch, noting the blinking red light on his display. "No, wait. Our tail section's out again."

"Anybody close enough to see us?" Stakem asked.

"There's nothing in the air close enough," Volland answered. "The area below us is pretty sparsely populated."

"All right," Stakem said. "We need to send a burst message to let our sponsor know where we're going down."

"I've got it," Volland answered.

Stakem kept the plane on autopilot as the fuel gauge registered zero. The grassland on the screen beneath the pilot's feet rushed past; the plane's long shadow stretched to the east, darting over hedges.

Within minutes, the image of a farm zoomed onto the screen ahead of the pilot. He disengaged the autopilot and carefully vectored the deflectors in the jet engine. The exhaust of the jets was diverted downward by the side nozzles and the plane's speed dropped. The machine's momentum continued to carry them forward for a short distance until they hung suspended on columns of hot gas over the abandoned farm. Stakem glanced at the fuel gauge; it was now well below zero and flashed an angry red.

"We've got a radar source coming up behind us," Volland warned.

Stakem checked the display. The computer hadn't identified the source but it appeared to be a low-flying helicopter.

"Our tail screen's still malfunctioning," Hauschild warned.

The pilot knew that if he didn't hurry, it was certain that the Superstealth would be spotted. He lowered the plane on its columns of hot gas, easing it forward until it was just a few meters from the old grain elevator. The wide doors of the barn-like elevator were both open, promising sanctuary if the pilot could somehow get the plane into the building before the helicopter overtook them.

"They're coming up fast!" Volland shouted. "It's an SA-330."

The pilot eased the Superstealth forward. The plane's engines sputtered as the aircraft neared the hiding place. The nose eased into the dark opening and then unexpectedly the plane shuddered as the right wing hung up on the door frame.

Stakem shoved forward on the control stick. There was a rending of wood as the door frame of the grain elevator gave way. The plane waffled into the darkness of the interior. The wheels scraped along the dirt floor and then came to a stop.

"Where are they?" Stakem asked, his display screen having gone blank. "Did they see us?"

"I don't think so," Volland said.

Stakem closed his eyes and leaned back in his seat. Above the grain elevator, the French SA-330 Puma went thundering by.

5

Oz and his men spent several hours being debriefed, first by the French military, then by American Army Intelligence personnel, and finally by the security staff from Osbourn-Norton. But the Night Stalkers had little information that helped the ongoing search for the Superstealth.

At twenty-two hundred hours the debriefings were completed and word came that the French Military's search for the Superstealth had proven to be fruitless. Oz received orders to remain in the "safe house" the American Embassy had utilized to conduct the debriefing of the Night Stalkers. Exhausted, Oz had slept in a Louis XIV chair in one corner of a high-ceilinged room.

"Good morning, Sleeping Beauty," a familiar voice awakened him.

"Grant?" Oz asked, and then groaned from the pain in his stiff neck as he turned to see the CIA agent standing in the arched doorway of the room.

"Who'd you expect?" Larry Grant asked around a smoldering cigar that smelled so bad it turned Oz's stomach. The agent had a muscular frame, and the jagged scar on his left cheek hinted at his military background. He wore a crumpled gray suit and dress shirt without a tie. In the past, Grant and Oz had worked on several missions together, becoming close friends, although neither would have admitted it.

Oz looked at his watch and swore. "I need to get some rest. We have another demonstration flight this morning at—"

"Been canceled," Grant said, ambling into the room. "You're assigned to help me for the duration. The Army's flying three more Night Stalkers teams over for backup in case we get a lead on the Superstealth and I came in on the Concorde this morning when we finally got word that the French had muffed finding the plane. From what I hear, things got pretty exciting yesterday. You had anything to eat?"

"It's midnight," Oz grimaced. "Are we talking supper or breakfast?"

"Well, I'm on Washington time—more like supper for me and breakfast for you. I got some rolls and coffee at the all-night restaurant down the street," Grant said, holding up a white paper sack.

The CIA agent sauntered over to an ornate, gold-leafed table. The paper napkins he tossed onto its polished marble surface looked out of place. He gingerly removed two styrofoam cups of coffee from the sack and popped the lids off them.

"We've got some people studying the gadget somebody wired into your chopper," Grant said as he smashed his cigar into an ashtray lying on the table. "That was some piece of work. They tell me you're lucky to be alive."

"You mean somebody sabotaged the MH-60K?" Oz asked incredulously as he pulled a chair up to the table and sat down.

"It was wired into the autopilot. If the thing hadn't malfunctioned, you'd never have regained control of your chopper. From what Death Song told me, you just about got creamed as it was."

"That's no lie," Oz declared. "You think that's connected to the theft of the Superstealth?" The pilot tore a plastic container open and dumped cream into his coffee.

"It'd be quite a coincidence if the two weren't connected. But no one can come up with a logical reason why they are. Making you crash during the exhibition would've brought in that many more authorities—something whoever stole the plane wouldn't have wanted. And there's no way they could have known you'd break up their party when they were trying to steal the Superstealth."

"So you think the two are unrelated?" Oz asked around a lemon pudding-filled donut.

"That's my gut feeling."

"I suppose that's possible," Oz nodded. "The Sikorsky helicopters are being purchased by more and more countries. There're plenty of competitors who wouldn't mind seeing one of Sikorsky's best models crash at the Paris Air Show."

"That'd leave a lasting impression on potential buyers," Grant agreed. "In the meantime, we're going to try to trace some of the components that were incorporated into the device. But I'm not too optimistic that we'll get anywhere."

"That leaves us with tracking down the Super-stealth?"

"Right," Grant said, licking the sugar off his fingers. "Spain, Belgium, Italy—most of Europe—are all helping in the search. But, frankly, we're going to be real lucky if anybody comes up with anything. No radar signature, no possibility of visual sightings—it's going to be tough."

"Yeah," Oz agreed. "I suppose anybody that went to all the work of stealing the thing had a good way to conceal it."

"There is one hopeful bit of information," Grant said, gulping his coffee. "The Osbourn-Norton company rep says he doesn't think they were able to refuel the Superstealth before you guys forced it to take off. If that's true, he told me they didn't have enough fuel to get out of France. Osbourn-Norton had ordered the ground crew to keep the tanks only partially full just in case they had trouble during the air show and were forced to make an emergency landing."

"Sounds like all the bugs weren't worked out of the design," Oz said. "Maybe that's why they weren't able to outdistance us yesterday."

"I get the impression there're still some bugs in the system. Anyway, the fuel's a special high-octane brew; regular jet fuel apparently gums up the engine in a hurry."

"But if they were forced to land somewhere in France . . ."

"Then the jet's probably hidden somewhere on the ground right here in France," Grant completed his thought.

"But how could they hide the plane?"

"Good question. But these guys made some good plans. They might have succeeded in hiding the plane from air surveillance."

Oz was silent as he sipped his coffee.

Grant continued, "Also, the rep said the French government required a minimal amount of nuclear fuel to be carried in the jet's on-board reactor during its flights at the air show."

"Nuclear fuel would be hard to obtain," Oz remarked. "But without it, the plane wouldn't be much more than a regular stealth aircraft—hardly worth stealing."

"Yeah. They need the fuel if the aircraft is to be of any value to anyone. I've got some of my people tracking down possible sources of fuel and reactor materials now. In the meantime, I've got a meeting lined up in about an hour with somebody who wants to sell us some information. We've dealt with this source before, but the information isn't always reliable. Want to tag along?"

"Sure," Oz answered, putting down his empty cup.

Grant lit a match and puffed another cigar to life. He blew a cloud of smoke into the air as he tossed the match into the ashtray. "I've gotten you temporary diplomatic status while you're working with me; that way you can carry a concealed weapon and not have to worry about getting caught with it. Whoever stole this plane is playing for keeps. Each of the ground crew in the Superstealth hangar had been shot in the back of the head. We found the weapons control and electronic countermeasures engineers there, too. The pilot's missing; he may have been in on the deal. Osbourn-Norton says it would take at least two crew members to get the plane into the air.''

"So somebody had at least one guy trained to help fly the experimental plane.''

"Right,'' Grant said. He checked his watch and then got to his feet. "We better get going if we're going to meet my contact. You've got your Ruger, I see. Better bring it along.''

Oz climbed out of the beat-up taxi that had taken them to a seedy street halfway across Paris. After Grant paid the driver, the two Americans found themselves on a garishly-lit street filled with people, rich and poor, enjoying a night of revelry. Snippets of different languages and dialects assaulted Oz's ears. There was a cascade of mad laughter in the distance, followed by the smashing of a bottle against the pavement.

The air was cool, coated with the smells of exotic perfumes and foods, and just a hint of the stench of garbage. The businesses along the avenue varied from peep shows to discos, as blaring music invaded the street.

Grant dodged three androgenous teenagers and walked toward a queue of a dozen people, waiting to enter a show. Oz fell into place at the end of the line behind a couple that stood arm in arm. The line fed into a gaudily lit archway glowing with flickering neon lights.

"See the Forgotten Paris," flashed a sign flanked by grinning skulls.

"This way," the guide billed as "Monsieur Morte" told the small crowd as he opened a metal gate to admit them. "Straight ahead and through the door," the guide directed, locking the gate behind them with a snap that sounded like a shot on the silent street beyond.

"This place always spooks me," the young man in front of Oz admitted to his girlfriend, who still had her arm around him.

The line of people followed the guide down limestone flagstones that were worn from a century of use. At the end of the walkway, Monsieur Morte unlatched a heavy iron and wooden door. It swung open on squeaky hinges to reveal a dimly-lit stairwell leading downward. "Watch your step, s'il vous plaît," he warned.

Oz followed the couple down the steep alabaster steps in the arched passageway of crudely dressed stones. One of the tourists far in front whispered something, and the fat man beside him snickered.

The guide flipped a switch at the base of the steps, lighting the archway that led into the dimly-lit passage.

As the tourists followed the guide along the narrow hall, Oz was startled to realize that what he had thought were stone fragments lining the walls were actually rows of neatly stacked human bones. What had appeared to be piles of cobblestones were, in fact, stained skulls. A few were bleached white, but most were brown; here and there the bones were blackened as if they had been burned long ago. Bones resting against the limestone ceiling bore patches of azure mineral deposits like cancerous growths.

"Ladies and gentlemen," Monsieur Morte said after all had entered the narrow hall. "We're in what we in Paris call the 'Empire of Death.'" His hushed voice echoed down the long cavern. "This is part of the Paris Catacombs, a place many tourists don't even realize exists."

There was a loud rattling beside them. Oz fought the urge to reach for the pistol hidden under his jacket.

The tour guide flicked the beam of his flashlight toward the disturbance. A large rat with jeweled red eyes glared at them. The woman in front of Oz laughed nervously.

"As you can see," the guide said, "we are not the only ones interested in the bones. Now, if you'll come this way."

The line of people trudged on, Grant and Oz continuing to bring up the rear of the line.

It was several minutes before the guide spoke again. "Like other large European cities, the cemeteries of Paris have been overcrowded for centuries. During the last two hundred years, the most ancient of the graves have been exhumed and the bones transferred into the labyrinth of old quarries that lie under the city. Some of these bones date back to the French Revolution. Others are even older."

Oz shuddered involuntarily as he eyed the skulls piled on top of one another like bricks; behind the wall of craniums, the flickering lights revealed piles of humerus, femur, and other smaller bones, stacked like firewood. The brown skulls lined the poorly lit passageway as far as Oz could see into the darkness.

"How big is this place?" the fat man asked after they'd marched silently along the bone-lined passageway for several more minutes.

"It extends for miles," the guide answered. "There are over six million bodies interred here."

"And I'd be willing to bet there are some newer corpses hidden down here, too," Grant muttered around his cigar. "We're almost there," he warned Oz. "Stay close to me."

As the guide led the tourists on, Grant side-stepped down a narrow hall leading in a different direction. Oz followed the agent. Their path was lit by a string of dusty bulbs hanging from the ceiling ahead of them.

"Bon soir, Monsieur Grant," a soft, feminine voice whispered from the shadows.

"Bon soir, Mademoiselle," Grant replied.

Oz studied the woman who slinked out of the darkness. Her large, dark eyes were outlined with heavy mascara and her pinkish hair was spiked with so much hair gel it appeared wet. She wore tight blue jeans and a leather jacket. A tiny silver skull pin, held in place by a stud, graced her left nostril.

Grant approached the woman. The agent took an envelope from inside his jacket.

The woman reached for the envelope but Grant pulled it back out of her reach. "First, what have you got for me?"

She was silent a moment before speaking. "C'est rumored that arms merchants stole la Superstealth," she said in a thickly accented mixture of French and English.

"We figured that much," Grant said, exasperated. "Who's responsible for the theft?"

"L'Artillerie de Rotterdam was hired to steal la Superstealth."

"Artillerie Rotterdam?"

"Oui."

"How could that be? They manufacture pistols for the government. There's no way—"

"I just report what I hear," the woman interrupted, veiling her eyes with her long lashes.

"And where do you hear these things?" Grant asked.

"That I will not reveal. Now do you want to hear what I have?"

"Go on."

"They refueled outside Beaumont then hopped to Rotterdam."

Grant chewed on his cigar for a moment. "All right. Anything else?"

"The plane is to be sold to a Chinese buyer. I know no more. You must offrir un cadeau." She held out her hand.

Grant handed her the envelope.

"Merci bien," she said with a pout.

"Let me know if you hear anything else."

She smiled, then turned and sauntered away without looking back, vanishing around a bony corner and melting into the darkness. Her high-heeled boots echoed into the distance.

"Rotterdam," Grant said. "Doesn't sound right, to me."

The two Americans turned to retrace their steps.

Oz pulled his collar up to counter the chill air of the passageway and then spoke. "Rotterdam wasn't in the general direction the Superstealth was headed for when we started to follow them. But they did turn and head in that direction as they eluded the French fighters."

Grant blew another cloud of smoke from his cigar. "So there's an outside chance they were headed for Rotterdam. But it puzzles me that Artillerie Rotterdam would be involved. We haven't had any indication that anybody in the Netherlands has been dealing on the black market. And it's one thing to sell arms. But a plane? I can't imagine they're set up for it."

The CIA agent puffed on his cigar, lost in thought as the two made their way out of the bone-lined passageway toward the streets of Paris above them.

Although the information Grant had purchased didn't jive with what the CIA data bank showed on Artillerie Rotterdam, it was all they had to go on. The easiest solution to the problem would have been for the authorities in the Netherlands to simply inspect the Artillerie Rotterdam plant to see if the Superstealth was hidden there.

But the Dutch government refused to conduct or condone a search of the Artillerie Rotterdam, apparently because one of the company's board of directors was a cousin to Claus Von Enkhuberg, Holland's new prince.

The CIA therefore decided to take covert action of its own to determine whether the Superstealth was hidden in the Artillerie Rotterdam complex. Soon Grant and Oz were flying the CIA's Learjet toward Rotterdam.

6

The two muscular men circled warily, scrutinizing each other for some sign of the attack that was inevitable. Naked from the waist up, their muscular bodies were drawn taut in readiness. The flickering fluorescent bulb in the small room made a low-pitched drone that was broken only by the sound of their deep breathing. The fluorescent light was reflected from the blades of the razor-sharp combat knives each man held.

Suddenly Gavrilovich Degtyarev lunged. His blade nearly grazed the balding scalp of Sergei Federov who dodged to one side. The knife slashed the empty air where he had been.

Federov waited a moment, then countered with an upward jab that would have been a fatal, disemboweling cut had he followed through with it. He spoke softly in his native Russian, "That's once."

Degtyarev wiped the sweat out of his eye with his free hand, wiggling the fingers on the other hand that grasped the dagger. He took a step forward, dropping to one knee as he lunged unexpectedly, his blade stabbing at his opponent's groin.

Federov swiftly dodged to the left, his opponent's blade again cutting into the empty air where he had been. As Federov sidestepped, his right leg flew into the air, hitting Degtyarev in the leg and knocking him down. Federov reached toward his fallen opponent; his blade nicked Degtyarev's exposed back. "That's two," Federov said, dancing out of reach as Degtyarev slashed with fury at the shorter man's legs.

Degtyarev slowly got to his knees, ignoring the minor pain from the small cut on his back. He seemed to rest a moment, as if his strength were almost exhausted.

There was the click of a door behind Federov. He turned toward the sound.

Instantly, Degtyarev flexed his coiled muscles and launched himself into the air with snake-like quickness. The blade in his hand was a mirrored blur as he struck savagely at his opponent's legs.

Federov jumped straight into the air as the blade darted out. He leaped over the slashing attack and then dodged the counter chop that followed, narrowly missing his stomach and thighs.

For a moment Degtyarev was off balance and stumbled into a crouching position. Federov kicked once more. His booted foot caught Degtyarev's hand; the dagger spun from his hand and clattered across the floor. Another kick and Degtyarev fell onto his back with a groan, closing his eyes in pain.

Degtyarev opened his eyes to find Federov's blade hovering over his exposed neck, only a fraction of an inch from his pulsating jugular vein. Degtyarev froze, not daring to move.

"Three," Federov whispered, withdrawing his weapon and slamming it into the scabbard on his belt.

Gavrilovich Degtyarev rose to his feet and crouched, both hands outstretched, refusing to admit defeat.

Federov smiled. "Very good comrade, very good. But it is enough. Time to quit."

"Major Federov," the voice of General Simonov spoke from the shadows of the room. "I need a word with you."

"Yes, General," Federov answered. He turned to Degtyarev. "I will see you later."

As Federov turned back toward him, the general said, "Your daily workouts have honed your skills—and those of your men—to a level I would have thought unattainable. I want you to come with me. I have a task that will put other of your skills to the test." He lowered his voice and added, "We have a lead on the missing American plane."

KGB officer Federov quickly pulled on a green sweatshirt emblazoned with a small red star, and followed the general out into a drab hallway. Uniformed soldiers and secret police in cheap black suits hurried up and down the corridor. The general's leather boots clicked on the marble floor as he spoke. "You were briefed yesterday on the traffic we'd intercepted over Paris. The French have still not located the stolen Superstealth. This morning our Paris bureau has reported a flurry of activity in the American Embassy."

Major Federov mulled over what the general had said. He unconsciously rubbed the balding scalp that made him look more like a friar than a KGB agent. He had an innocent, even bumbling look, but mistaking Federov's harmless appearance for his personality had cost more than one man his life. "So the West has no idea where the American high-tech jet has gone?" Federov finally spoke.

"That is correct," the general replied. "No one in the West has any idea where the American toy is. But we do."

"But where did we get such information?" Federov asked, astonished.

"The computers we've been buying from the Japanese are starting to pay off," the general said as he opened a tall door at the end of the hall and entered.

A mousey-looking bureaucrat jumped to attention as the two officers strode into the waiting room of the general's office.

The man spoke hurriedly, "General, the forms we sent over—"

"Later, later," the general said briskly, dismissing the little man with a wave of his hand. "We have important things to do." The general opened the door to his office.

Major Federov and General Simonov entered the office. The general closed the door behind himself before the man could do more than murmur a vain protest.

"Paper pushers is what the Americans call them," the general said, shaking his head as he crossed the paneled room and sat down in the creaking chair behind his desk. "There're scrambling trying to make more work for themselves before

they're all replaced by computers and budget cuts."
The general flashed a wicked smile that displayed a
gold tooth. "Losing a few more paper pushers will
make the belt tightening for our new five-year eco-
nomic plan all the more worthwhile.

"Now," he continued as Federov settled his
muscled frame into one of the wooden chairs in front
of the general's desk. "As to what we've found. A
search of our data banks revealed a report from the
Gavrilovich Arms plant. The report is interesting in
light of yesterday's events."

"Gavrilovich?" Federov asked. "That's one of
our new arms plants aimed at commercial sales?"

"Right," General Simonov answered, leaning
back in his chair. "If Stalin could see us today he'd
probably have the Supreme Soviet shot. Working
like capitalists to manufacture quality products to sell
to sportsmen and Third World dictators . . . Anyway,
Gavrilovich's arms division was contacted by a man
offering to sell Superstealth technology to them. At
the time the offer was viewed as a hoax and dismissed."

"But now it appears there might have been
something to it," Federov commented.

"Exactly." The general sat up and extracted a
key from his pocket. He quickly unlocked his desk
and yanked a manila folder from it. "Here's the file.
I don't need to tell you what getting such technologi-
cal secrets might do to help our aircraft manufacturers."

Federov opened the folder and inspected the
contents for a moment. "So you want me to contact
the man and obtain photos and schematics?"

"My superiors are hoping we can do more than that. Since the aircraft can be flown without being detected . . ." He said no more.

Federov glanced toward the general and smiled, showing his crooked teeth. "Yes. I think I understand." He looked back at the folder he held.

"As you can see, the contact was in Paris," the general said.

"That would seem to tie into the events of the last few days as well. So I'm going to Paris?"

"Correct. Immediately. Get showered and dressed. I'll dispatch this folder along with an aide shortly; you can read the report on the way to the airport and he will return it to me. You'll travel with a civilian passport. We already have a Voyenno Vozdushnize Sily helicopter team in Paris. Major Komonsky is there flying our new Mi-35."

"Major *Peter* Komonsky?" Federov asked, handing the folder back to the general.

"One and the same," General Simonov smiled. "The pilot that got your ass out of Ethiopia last summer."

"Excellent," Federov said, recalling his nearly fatal assignment in Africa. "He's the best man for the job. No one can out-fly him."

"He's got his handpicked crew there with him. We'll have the Mi-35 he's been flying at the Paris Air Show on standby for you as well."

"Armament?"

"Our embassy will supply you with a 'sanitized' Czech CZ-75. We've also got munitions in Paris for the helicopter if things become really serious."

"Good." Federov placed the folder back on the general's desk.

"Our KGB agents in Paris will be at your disposal," the general continued. "Be discreet but remember that if you can get the plane, the new technology could give us what we need to jump ahead of the Americans as well as the Japanese and their new fighter jet program."

Federov rose to his feet. "I have no questions."

"Good luck, then."

7

Rotterdam lay in the *polders,* the region which had been created by the series of dikes. The city was an island of industry built in the center of rich farmland that had once been at the bottom of the ocean. The metropolis had one of the world's busiest harbors. Its shipyards and airports worked at full capacity loading and unloading goods destined for all parts of the globe. The city itself had a reputation, even among the hard-working Dutch, as being all business; the saying among Hollanders was that shirts sold in Rotterdam had the sleeves already rolled up.

With the fertile *polders* land at a premium, the modern city had many high-rises; apartment buildings often bridged over busy streets to make the best possible use of space. The buildings themselves were new, most of them having been built since World War II, when German bombs had leveled the metropolis. Oddly shaped, futuristic architecture was the norm in the city, rather than the exception.

Oz and Grant had arrived at the airport north of Rotterdam at three-thirty AM. Once they were clear of metal detectors, Grant produced a key to one of the lockers at the airport and removed a large suitcase. The agent searched in the parking lot until he found a blue Volvo. He placed the suitcase on the trunk of the car and, checking to be sure no one was watching, opened the case.

He reached in and quickly retrieved two pairs of rubber surgical gloves. "Put these on and wear them until we're ready to leave," he directed Oz. Grant carefully wiped the suitcase down with his handkerchief. "We don't want to leave any fingerprints behind if we have to abandon this car or any of our equipment. And be sure I don't smoke. Cigars can be checked for saliva. The new DNA techniques would enable them to identify me from a stub."

Oz wriggled his fingers into the gloves. Grant produced another pair of keys that fit the Volvo's locks. The two Americans climbed into the car with Grant behind the wheel.

The CIA agent started the car, backed it out of its parking space and drove toward the Artillerie Rotterdam complex. "Open the suitcase," he said.

Oz released the two studs on the suitcase and lifted the lid. Inside, he found two old 1911A1 automatic handguns, spare magazines for them, and their .45 ACP ammunition. Also in the suitcase were a pair of binoculars, electronic gear, and a silencer which fitted on the threaded barrel of one of the pistols. All the gear was carefully fitted into a foam lining designed to protect it.

"We'll have to be real careful not to get caught with these," Grant said, turning the corner onto a narrow street. "You're better off dealing hard drugs here in Holland than getting caught with a pistol.

They're liberal about everything *except* firearms. The guns can't be traced, so don't be afraid to ditch them if you get cornered by the authorities."

Grant parked the Volvo on the street opposite the Artillerie Rotterdam plant at the northern edge of the city and turned off the car lights. The two men loaded the weapons in the darkness and jammed the guns into their belts. Rather than go directly to the industrial complex, the Americans broke through the thin barrier at the front of the construction site next to their car.

Soon they were on top of the skeletal building under construction, which would remain abandoned until the sun rose. The height of the unlit structure allowed them to easily study the large industrial complex opposite them without being observed.

A warm breeze laden with moisture swept across the construction site for a moment, making a low droning sound in the cable lift next to them. Oz handed the binoculars back to Grant. "Artillerie Rotterdam looks all but abandoned."

"That's to be expected at four AM," Grant answered quietly as he raised the optics to his eyes. "Most manufacturers in this country don't run night shifts. Despite the hard work the Dutch put in during the day, Rotterdam always seems to die at nightfall. Factories and shops close up and everyone heads home."

The nearly empty factory across from them was almost totally dark, with only a few floodlights illuminating the chain-link fence surrounding it. "All I see are the two guards at the front gate and the foot patrol that passed ten minutes ago on this side of the plant," Grant finally said. "The delivery gate at the west isn't even being watched, as far as I can tell. It doesn't look like they have any sensors or cameras on the grounds."

"Doesn't that seem odd for an arms plant?"

"Real odd. Something hasn't felt right about this whole thing right from the start."

The two men were quiet for a moment as the cable droned again in the wind.

"The west fence looks like our best bet to me," Oz finally said.

"Yeah, me too," Grant agreed. He swept it once more with the binoculars. "There're a bunch of places the Superstealth could be hidden."

"Let's try inside the large building south of the tower," Oz suggested. "They might have squeezed it in there or into that building next to it. But I can't believe they have good enough secrecy for their regular workers not to know about the plane if it's down there."

"That makes sense. It'd have to be in a building that's pretty secure." The CIA agent folded his binoculars and placed them into his jacket pocket.

"It would narrow our search considerably, if we didn't have to check the regular assembly lines."

"In theory," Grant agreed. "But if the plane's *not* down there, we could end up searching the whole plant just to be sure. There's no way the two of us can do that in a couple of hours."

"Then we'd better get started."

The two Americans crept to a darkened section of the fence where a floodlight had burned out. Oz used wire cutters to hack an opening along the lower edge of the fence and then dropped to his stomach to crawl through the small opening.

As he started to wriggle under the fence, Grant grabbed his shoulder. "Hang on," he whispered. The agent pointed to a small box behind the fence.

"Sensor?"

"Yeah. Lasers."

Oz crawled back out as Grant fished a tiny instrument from his pocket. "It's probably a new pulsed system with multiple beams. This is going to take a couple of minutes to work out, so keep a sharp lookout."

Oz rose to his feet and checked up and down the fence. His eyes narrowed at a movement about a hundred yards away, near the corner of the plant's fence. He watched the area and saw the movement again. "See someone there," Oz whispered to Grant.

"Where?"

"Down the way. Right there!"

Both men watched the movement and then Oz swore under his breath as a cocker spaniel darted into the road along the fence.

Grant turned back to his work. He carefully snaked the small device through the cut in the fence. Lying prone, the agent cautiously shoved the box into the path the invisible laser had to take to get to the sensor post ten feet away. When a small red LED on the box started to blink, the agent instantly froze.

The red light continued to blaze for thirty seconds, then went out, replaced by a green LED. Grant sighed with relief since the green light signaled that the small laser and computer chip inside the box were now duplicating the frequency-modulated pattern used by the sensors in the burglar alarm.

The agent waited a moment, then slowly nudged the box toward the right; the green LED continued to shine.

"OK," Grant whispered to Oz. "Stay low and to the left of the box. And don't move quickly until you're clear of the sensors. I'll go first."

Oz waited while Grant wriggled under the fence and inched his way through the invisible laser beams of the sensors. After the CIA agent was several yards past the sensor, he rose in the shadows and beckoned to Oz.

The pilot dropped to his belly and wormed his way under the fence, slowly inching toward Grant's feet which were about all he could see ahead of him.

"Freeze," Grant hissed.

Oz slowly turned his head and glanced back at his feet, which were barely visible through the fence. The brown cocker spaniel had its head in the hole in the wire, just inches from Oz's feet.

"Don't move, I'm going to shoot it," Grant whispered, pulling his silenced .45 from under his jacket.

"Wait," Oz said. He gave a quick, brutal kick that caught the dog in the nose. The animal yelped, scrambled out of the hole, and raced away. With the toe of his boot, Oz bent the wire fence back together so the animal couldn't crawl through later if it came back. Oz turned back onto his belly and continued crawling toward Grant, who was replacing his pistol in his belt.

"I just hope the whole world didn't hear it yelping," Grant whispered as Oz rose to his feet beside him. "Soft-hearted pilots are always suckers for hound dogs. Come on."

Oz followed the agent as they crept through the shadows toward the large storehouse they hoped to inspect first. As they rounded the corner and quickly crossed to the entrance of the building, a figure on the cat walk above them shifted his MP5SD silenced submachine gun and lifted a small Motorola Radius P10 radio to his lips. He spoke softly in Dutch into the mouthpiece of the radio: "Our birds are almost in the snare." He didn't wait for a reply. Instead he switched off the radio and turned to those beside him. "Get ready."

"We're nearing the coast," the pilot of the M-78 warned Waeytens over the intercom. The dark ocean raced below them, the aircraft almost skimming its surface. "I'm taking us off TF/TA radar. ETA is ten minutes."

"All right," Waeytens replied. "Go in low; we can't afford to be detected by the military."

Leo Waeytens had planned his course of action as carefully as any military commander had ever planned a battle. The nuclear breeder reactor had been carefully reconnoitered for nearly a month; Waeytens' team had rehearsed their attack on the complex again and again.

The paramilitary force consisted of 25 men, most of whom were ex-French Foreign Legionnaires. On paper, the men were hired to demonstrate the capabilities of small arms marketed by their employer—a job they regularly did with great skill at military shows around the world. What no one outside the Jouniaux empire knew was that the team was also utilized to do dirty work for the company. From time to time the ex-soldiers eliminated the company's competition or pirated equipment and materials that suppliers refused to sell at reasonable prices.

Like Waeytens, each man in the team carried an unregistered JAR-98 rifle. The rifle fired caseless, tracer cartridges fed from a 300-round magazine located in the weapon's stock. The JAR-98 was equipped with a sophisticated sighting system; it could fire in 5-round bursts, or in a continuous automatic mode, making it one of the most deadly small arms ever created. Three of the rifles, including the one Waeytens carried, had three-shot 30mm grenade launchers mounted underneath their rifle barrels.

The team rode in an M-78 transport helicopter. The aircraft was similar to the U.S. Military's CH-46 "Chinook" in layout, with a two-man crew and the capability of carrying a 25-man fighting force along with their combat loads.

The M-78 had Kawasaki M107-II turbo-engines both fore and aft, each of which powered a three-blade, 15.5 meter radius rotor. The powerful assault chopper had a cruising speed of 140 knots and a chin-mounted 7.62mm chain gun connected to a forward-looking infrared sight operated by the helicopter's co-pilot.

The pilot flew the chopper on a roundabout path toward the Zeus III nuclear breeder reactor near Dover, England. He flew the M-78 along the flight path logged with Belgian authorities over the first leg of their trip, supposedly to deliver parts to the town of Adinker.

When they reached Adinker, they continued westward rather than landing, crossing the Strait of

Dover, taking a direct path to the Zeus III nuclear plant.

Now Waeytens stood in the swaying helicopter, holding on to his seat to maintain his balance as they neared the reactor. "ETA is ten minutes," he hollered to the men around him. "Lock and load."

Like the others in the passenger compartment, Waeytens thumbed the selector of his weapon into the "safe" position, then used the charging lever over the barrel of the gun to cycle a caseless cartridge into the JAR-98's internal cylinder. After checking to be sure its safety was engaged, Waeytens then chucked three of the fat cartridges designed for the grenade launcher into that half of his firearm.

The pilot of the M-78 took the helicopter into a steep, stomach-wrenching climb up and over the rocky limestone cliff ahead of them. Then he leveled out to skim along the rolling grassland that led to the ridge overlooking the power plant.

"No radar signals," the navigator informed Waeytens. "Two minutes to landing."

Waeytens turned to the man beside him. "Open the side door," he commanded. He motioned to the man next to the other door to do the same. The two soldiers stood, their rifles hanging on slings over their shoulders, and carefully jerked the latches on the doors and slid them back. Warm air whipped through the passenger compartment as the doors were locked open.

Ahead of the chopper, the pilot sighted Zeus III. The concrete and steel containment building that rose 200 feet above the valley was dwarfed by the cooling tower that overshadowed it. To the right of the containment building was the white four-story building enclosing the plant's steam turbines. These generated electricity that was carried over the power lines leading toward distant London. Behind the containment structure was the fuel storage building.

"Masks," Waeytens ordered, pulling out his own gas mask from the pouch on his left thigh.

Every trooper pulled a similar M-200 gas mask from his pouch, hooked his thumbs into the sides of the mask, and expertly pulled the covering up and over his head. Each then tightened the straps and placed his hand over the intake valve, checking the air-tight seal of the mask.

Waeytens surveyed his troops through the narrow field of view offered by the eyepieces of his mask. While it was doubtful that those defending the reactor would have time to disperse tear gas, his men would be protected if it were employed.

He replaced the headset over his mask.

"—personnel," the navigator finished in the intercom as Waeytens got the headset into place.

"Say again," the team leader ordered awkwardly through the transceiver in the nosepiece of his mask.

"We've sighted the security personnel," the navigator repeated to Waeytens.

"Fire at will," Waeytens ordered.

The pilot dropped the M-78 slightly to adhere to a nap-of-the-earth flight as he approached the nuclear power plant. The complex was circled by a high chain-link fence topped by razor-sharp ribbon wire. The fence formed a large courtyard at the front of the plant, inside of which was a tractor trailer con-

taining a load of nuclear fuel. The single road leading to the reactor had a heavily fortified checkpoint
from which two guards now waved at the helicopter
as it swooped toward them.

They continued to smile and wave at the chopper, assuming it was on some type of military exercise. Only when the M-78's chin gun rotated toward
them did they realize something was amiss. As they
dashed for cover, the chin gun rattled out its attack,
efficiently cutting down one and then the other before either could reach safety.

The gunner then turned his weapon toward the
power and phone lines, blasting the glass insulators
holding the lines to their four-footed, high-tension
poles. The stream of bullets ripped the electrical
lines to pieces, shattering the insulators and sending
their wires to the ground in a shower of sparks. The
lines snaked and jumped as the electrical charges in
the wires violently leaked into the ground. Within
moments the lines shorted out, tripping circuit
breakers in the power plant and then hanging limp
and lifeless.

The pilot of the M-78 kicked his left rudder
pedal slightly to angle the chopper toward the open
courtyard ahead of them. As he had done in numerous exercises, the gunner raked the grounds of the
nuclear reactor with gunfire, killing or wounding
three workers who chanced to be in the open as the
helicopter approached.

"We're taking hits from somewhere," the pilot
said over the intercom.

"On the right," the navigator yelled. "My gun's
out of ammunition. I can't handle it."

"I've got it," Waeytens said over the intercom. He gazed out the window and spotted the guard who was firing from the top of the fuel storage building, half obscured by the containment shielding. Waeytens stepped toward the open side door. The man next to the door held on to Waeytens's combat vest as the leader aimed his grenade launcher at the guard.

The weapon recoiled violently in Waeytens's hands as the grenade was expelled from it. Before it landed, he fingered the semiauto launcher's trigger again, not wanting to take the chance of missing his target.

The first grenade landed near the man on the roof. Its concussion knocked him over. The second warhead landed directly on top of him, the force of the blast ripping him in two.

"More ground fire!" the navigator yelled over the intercom. "From the far west end of the plant, along the fence."

Waeytens tapped the trooper sitting next to the door, pointed, and hollered, "Take him, Bern."

The scar-faced soldier nodded and raised his weapon, his thumb snapping the selector into its automatic mode as he stood. The soldier next to him held on to Bern's combat vest as the helicopter lurched in the air. Bern pulled the trigger; the paths of his bullets were etched into the air by red tracer trails.

Bern adjusted his aim, watching the tracer trails, and almost instantly acquired the guard below the helicopter. The man seemed to be bathed for a moment in the stream of fire and then dropped to one knee.

The M-78 dropped unexpectedly and Bern lost his target for a moment. The guard rose to his feet and staggered toward the containment building. The attacker pulled the trigger again. This time the first rounds were on target and the guard fell headlong onto the concrete pavement.

"I'm setting us down," the pilot warned over the intercom as he brought the control column to its center position so the M-78 hovered over the clearing inside the fence. He pressed on the collective pitch lever with his left hand. The helicopter dropped to the ground, bouncing on its hydraulic landing gear, which absorbed much of the shock of the landing.

Waeytens jumped from the chopper, followed by his men. They spread out around the chopper in squads of five. Four of the squads guarded the helicopter and watched the buildings to be sure more armed guards didn't pose a threat. One squad charged toward the truck in the center of the compound.

Without warning there was an explosion of gunfire from the north end of the complex as a guard gripping an Enfield light support weapon fired from the hip. He scoured the troops who had disembarked from the right side of the M-78.

Three of Waeytens's men fell under the withering gunfire before the machine gun exhausted its 30-round magazine. There was a thunder of answering fire which erupted from the troops who remained standing on that side of the helicopter. The guard was cut to pieces before his body struck the pavement.

"Get them aboard," Waeytens ordered two of his men, indicating the casualties. No one could be left behind, since they might be identified by the authorities.

Waeytens watched as his men carried out their orders. He was unaware of the remote camera located atop the containment building. The automatic device was coupled with an auto ranger that filmed anything which moved in front of the containment building. The battle that had raged moments before had been recorded on the VCR connected to the surveillance camera.

Waeytens's fifth squad ignored the containment plant and other buildings, concentrating on breaking into the transport truck parked near the fuel storage building.

The soldiers quickly defeated the lock on the steel rear doors of the truck using a thermite grenade that produced a shower of molten steel as it burned. After knocking the melted lock out of the way with the barrel of a rifle, the men jerked the heavy doors ajar and climbed into the trailer.

Inside the dark trailer was a heavy shelf that looked like a wine rack; it contained forty metal canisters the size of loaves of bread. The men strode toward the locking mechanism that secured the rack and cut it with a second thermite grenade. They freed the heavy canisters of Pu-239 from the rack and carried the containers of fissionable plutonium from the truck.

Although the radioactive material inside the

containers was dangerous, the steel canisters were perfectly safe to handle since their metal bodies stopped the alpha particles emanating from the plutonium. The men carefully carted the canisters into the waiting M-78. They secured them in the specially designed heavy steel trunk located at the back of the passenger compartment.

Within minutes, the squad had twenty canisters loaded into the waiting chopper. The steel trunk containing the canisters was locked and the squad leader turned and gave Waeytens a thumbs-up signal.

We've got enough nuclear power to fuel the Superstealth's cloaking circuits for years, Waeytens thought to himself, quickly lifting his mask and wiping the sweat from his eyes. He brought a steel whistle to his lips and blew a long blast that carried over the roar of the M-78's rotors. Then he lowered his gas mask and climbed into the helicopter.

The team members raced back to the M-78 and jumped aboard. Waeytens quickly checked to be sure everyone was in the passenger compartment. Except for the empty seats of the three casualties, everyone was present. Waeytens refrained from glancing toward the three dead men stacked under a blood-stained tarp. Instead, he pulled his mask off and plugged his head set into the intercom.

"Let's go," he ordered.

The pilot lifted the cyclic pitch lever and the M-78 helicopter leaped into the air. He kicked the right rudder pedal to turn the helicopter about, then pushed the control column forward. The chopper raced away from the nuclear reactor buildings.

"No radar and no radio traffic," the navigator informed Waeytens.

"Good job," Waeytens told the crew. "We got in and out without being detected by the authorities. Everyone will be getting their bonus when we get back."

CHAPTER

9

Oz paused for a moment after he stepped into the darkened storehouse of the Artillerie Rotterdam complex.

Everything was perfectly still.

Then a soft but distinctive click. Without thinking, Oz shoved Grant to the side. Moments after the safety had been snapped off, there was the quiet clattering of a fast-cycling, silenced weapon accompanied by the thumping of bullets on the heavy metal door where Grant and Oz had stood.

Crouching in the darkness, Oz drew his 1911A1, snapping off its thumb safety as he brought it up. He could barely see the weapon's sights as he took careful aim at the figure standing in the open valley formed between two high mountains of stacked crates and boxes. Oz squeezed the trigger of his pistol.

There was a flash and the heavy recoil of the .45. Not waiting to see if he hit his target, Oz rolled along the floor, distancing himself from the point from which he'd fired, knowing his muzzle flash would give away his position.

Rising to his knees, Oz was satisfied to see a body lying on the floor where the attacker had been. The pilot looked around in the darkness and saw nothing. But there was a second quiet burst of a silenced automatic weapon that sent bullets bouncing off the concrete floor where Oz had been.

At least they don't have night vision goggles, Oz thought to himself. Otherwise the attackers would have known he was no longer where they were firing.

There was the scraping of boots. Oz looked up the scaffolding of a tall conveyor belt where the sound seemed to originate. He saw a flicker of movement, then two men silhouetted themselves against a skylight in the roof.

Big mistake, Oz thought to himself as he aimed his pistol. He fired four rapid shots, pausing momentarily between each one to recover from the recoil of the .45, using the muzzle flash to aim his next shot. He was satisfied to see both figures drop, one of them tumbling from the scaffolding to the concrete floor below.

Oz quickly dodged behind a nearby crate and exchanged the nearly empty magazine in his pistol for a full one. He pocketed the empty magazine. Eight, no ten cartridges left, he thought to himself. He'd have to make his shots count and then try for one of the submachine guns lying on the floor.

He listened carefully to the sounds in the dark building.

"Friendly coming in," Grant hissed as he dashed to the crate where Oz was concealed.

"See any more?" Oz asked.

"No. But then I didn't see the last two you aced until after you'd dropped them, either."

"They got sloppy. What now?"

Grant thought a moment. "I'm voting for a hasty retreat. We don't have much ammunition and the plant will be opening before long. If we can get out, we can call the police and tell them there're some shot-up bodies lying around this plant. They'll come racing in and do what the Dutch national authorities wouldn't: search the plant. We might get lucky and have the plane uncovered in the process."

"Sounds good to me," Oz whispered. "But we need to find another exit. I'm betting the door we came in's covered."

"Yeah, probably."

"Let's go right down this middle aisle. Anybody that's hidden in here is probably along the edge of the building. Once we're down to that intersection there under the skylight, we can cut toward the left until we reach the outside wall. If I remember right, there's an entrance somewhere around there."

"Good," Grant replied. "Let's leapfrog."

"I'll go first," Oz said. "Ready?"

"Go."

Oz dashed down the aisle, covering the bodies lying on the floor with his pistol as he ran. When he got even with the first one, he stooped and picked up the MP5SD, then ran a few more yards and stopped next to a forklift.

Catching his breath, Oz clicked the safety back up on his 1911A1 and pushed the pistol back into his belt. He checked the selector on the MP5SD with his thumb and then knelt, covering the aisle ahead of him with the submachine gun.

Grant ran silently past his position. Oz raised the barrel of the MP5SD, then turned to cover their rear. He glared into the darkness behind them and saw nothing. The pilot waited a moment for Grant to get into place and then turned and raced down the aisle. He passed Grant, who now was sheltered behind a fiberboard barrel along a tall stack of wooden crates.

Oz dropped to his knee at the intersection formed by his aisle and another. He looked to his left toward the dim light of the exit sign. As he watched, the pilot could see a figure with a rifle sneaking past the door. Oz raised his submachine gun and aimed the best he could in the darkness.

He expertly tapped the trigger of his weapon. It cycled a short burst, its mechanism making more noise than the blast muffled by its silencer. The empty brass cartridges tinkled onto the concrete floor; the target tumbled into a heap.

Grant came up to Oz's position and dropped to his knees on the opposite side of the aisle.

"Looks clear now," Oz whispered. Grant sprinted down the aisle a short distance and then crouched next to a crate resting on a small wheeled cart.

Oz took a deep breath and rushed for the exit. When he was halfway there, two figures jumped into the aisle in front of him, blocking his way.

Oz pulled the trigger on his weapon, firing from the hip. He dodged to his right, hoping to give Grant a clear shot.

The gunfire caught one of the figures in the knees. The man spun around and fell, writhing in pain.

The second man fired twice at Oz, the shots going wide. Grant's fire caught the man in the chest. The pilot jumped the bodies and continued his charge down the aisle. As he neared the door, he turned slightly so his hip slammed against the emergency release bar of the exit.

The door swung open, setting off an alarm that reverberated inside the building. It was answered with a wailing siren from outside the building. Oz hardly noticed the alarm. His attention was riveted on the three armed figures standing a short distance in front of him.

Oz again fired, spinning slightly at the hip. The blast from his submachine gun hit all three men. The MP5SD quit firing, even though Oz continued to pull its trigger.

He threw the empty submachine gun to the ground and pulled the 1911A1 from his belt, flicking off its thumb safety. He fired at the man with the pistol who was struggling to rise. The bullet connected; the man slumped to the ground.

Oz knelt to the side of the doorway as Grant came charging up behind him.

"Any more?" Grant asked.

"On that catwalk," Oz pointed far above them.

"Let me see . . ." Grant aimed carefully with the G3 rifle he'd picked up and fired twice. The two men on the metal bridge dropped.

Grant handed Oz the rifle. "I'm going through the fence where we entered. Cover me."

Oz held the weapon ready as he scanned the buildings around him. Grant stormed across the grassy section leading to the fence. When he reached the sensors, he dropped to his belly and wriggled past the laser alarms and through the chain-link fence.

As he motioned for Oz to follow, a dark figure rose from behind the Volvo parked across the street and took careful aim with a scoped, bolt-action sniper rifle. The CIA agent crouched, unaware of the danger behind him.

10

The din of the burglar alarm make it impossible for Oz to shout a warning to Grant. The sniper took careful aim at the CIA agent, who remained unaware of his presence.

Oz fought the urge to simply fire in the general direction of the attacker. Instead, he quickly shouldered his weapon, took careful aim, and fired.

Grant went into a crouch the moment he saw Oz shoulder the rifle. The agent stepped to one side, reaching for his pistol as he turned around. His movement forced the sniper across the street to shift his position as he rested his weapon on the car. While the sniper realigned his scope on Grant, Oz was able to fire.

Oz's bullet went wide of the sniper. But the crack of the passing projectile was shocking enough to make the sniper lose all thought of shooting. Instead, he dropped behind the safety offered by the car.

Grant charged the Volvo, his pistol in hand. Oz remained in place, using the door frame of the building he hid in to steady his hold on the rifle.

The sniper raised his head. Oz squeezed the trigger on the rifle.

The high-velocity 7.62mm bullet smashed into the man's forehead, killing him instantly. With the collision of the bullet, a fine mist of blood and tissue erupted from the hole the high-velocity slug created, splattering across the hood of the car as the man reeled backward.

Oz quickly glanced right and left to be sure there were no other threats. The sun was rising in the east, casting its dim light on the buildings of the complex. Oz saw nothing. He threw down the rifle and sprinted for the hole in the fence.

In the distance, the pilot could hear the falling wail of sirens. He dropped to his knees, then went prone to scramble under the fence. As he rose, he glanced down the street; in the distance were the flashing lights of approaching police cars.

Grant had the Volvo's engine running when Oz jerked the door open. As the pilot slid in, the agent released the clutch pedal and the car screeched away from the curb, leaving a trail of burnt rubber on the pavement.

As the Americans traveled at break-neck speed, they threw their weapons out the car window into the grass-covered ditch. They managed to avoid a police roadblock by circling around and driving along a gravel road. Once they had caught the main highway back to the airport, they were safe. They reached the airport without incident, quickly traveled through the metal detectors toward the section of the airport reserved for private planes, and got in their Learjet. Oz was exhausted and soon fell asleep as Grant flew the plane back toward Paris.

"The Dutch authorities have placed photos of the men found at the Artillerie Rotterdam on the wire," Grant told Oz as they entered what the CIA's Paris bureau called their "Intelligence Room."

The immense room had a patterned-tin ceiling and ornate door frames that betrayed the fact it was part of the two-hundred-year-old house. But otherwise the windowless room looked ultra-modern, with a bank of computerized workstations, data-transfer radios, and sophisticated coding/decoding equipment. The various workstations were surrounded with six-foot screens to offer privacy to those operating the machines.

"Becky's the computer genius here in Paris," Grant told Oz as they approached one of the IBM RISC System/6000 workstations, where a slender woman in her mid-twenties was tinkering with a keyboard.

"I heard that," the platinum blond said, flashing a quick smile at Grant. "And flattery will *not* get you anywhere."

"Becky, this is Oz. Oz, Becky Loren."

She wrinkled her pug nose at the helicopter pilot to say hello.

Her platinum blond hair fell loosely below her shoulders in ringlets. She had a model's sharp cheekbones and prominent chin. The effect was enhanced by the microskirt she wore, in keeping with current Paris fashions for spring. Her bare arms were thin but muscular, suggesting a fetish for exercise.

"Now before you heap any more compliments on me, tell me what you need," Becky said to Grant.

"I need to have you pull the faces of the men killed or wounded early this morning at the Artillerie Rotterdam." Grant pulled up a chair so he could watch the screen. Oz took a seat on the other side of Becky.

"Be on the Interpol wire, right?" Becky asked, flipping the screen on the workstation to another electronic window.

"Right. I just got word they were out." Grant started to light his cigar, then remembered the ban against smoking near the sensitive equipment in the room.

Becky's fingers flew along the workstation's keyboard. "I've got them, but it takes a couple of seconds for the electronics to reconstruct the digital data into photos," she explained as the screen remained blank. "It takes a lot of dots to make a photo."

One by one, the faces of the men—some obviously dead when photographed—appeared on the large computer screen. Several had been identified by Interpol and had their names and criminal records outlined below their photos. Three had not yet been identified. "Not a pretty bunch of guys," Becky commented as Grant studied the photos.

"Any word about a stolen jet being found in the plant?" Grant asked. "We were hoping the Superstealth might have been hidden there."

"They should have alerted us if they found the plane," Becky said. "I know we haven't had any cables on that."

"Maybe they didn't recognize what they found," Oz suggested. "The jet doesn't look too different from a standard fighter when the stealth circuits are off. Does Artillerie Rotterdam manufacture any aircraft?"

"Maybe the Superstealth was hidden in with them," Grant nodded.

"First let's make sure they didn't find any strange aircraft," Becky told them as she tapped some keys.

In a moment the English translation of the Rotterdam police report that had accompanied the photos dropped onto the screen, blotting out several of the photos.

Becky defined search parameters by typing "plane," "jet," and "Superstealth" into the computer. The machine quickly sorted through the data in the report and alerted her that there were no matches with the target words.

"That's a negative search," Becky said. "And according to the police, the whole plant was inspected. That line right there." She pointed to the screen.

"Do they make any type of jet there?" Grant asked. "There still might have been a mixup."

"Let's see." Becky punched a key, pulling down a second window that seemed to scroll over the photos and police report already on the screen. In a few minutes she had accessed a listing of the production figures and products of various European companies. She scanned through it for the Artillerie Rotterdam listing, then pulled it from the data she'd collected.

"Rocket engines and ammunition. They don't manufacture any type of planes or aircraft parts there."

"I was afraid of something like that," Grant said after studying the screen. "Okay. Let's go at things from a different angle. What's the background of the guys found in the plant?"

Becky hit a button that erased the reports, leaving the photos of the men on the screen. She typed in a search program and waited a few seconds. A list of common characteristics shared by the men appeared.

"Well," she laughed as she studied the list. "I don't suppose the fact that all but one had brown hair is too significant. But it looks like four of them have ties to, or are members of, the PRG."

Grant groaned. "The PRG. Then this is undoubtedly a wild-goose chase."

"What's the PRG?" Oz asked.

"The People's Revolutionary Guard," Becky supplied.

"The PRG is a bunch of losers trying to abolish capitalism and bring communism to—or back to—all of Europe," Grant added.

"Not too progressive given the current situation in Europe," Becky said with a smile.

"They certainly played for keeps at the Artillerie Rotterdam," Oz said.

"That they did," Grant agreed. "It would be wrong to think of them as harmless. They're *deadly* serious about bringing communism to Europe. But stealing the Superstealth is out of their league."

"Then what were they up too?" Oz asked.

"I'm betting it was a set up to make the U.S.

look bad," Grant answered. "They were probably planning on damaging the plant and leaving two American bodies behind to sour Dutch/American relations or some such thing. It's hard to say exactly what they really had planned, since they're not operating with an elevator that goes to the top floor. But you can be sure it was nothing good."

"So the Superstealth was a good way to sucker us?" Oz asked.

"That's where I'd put my money," Grant said.

"Where's that leave us?" Oz asked.

"At a dead end until something else turns up," Grant answered, fighting the urge to smoke his cigar.

"There might be another way to track the people who stole the Superstealth," Oz said as he rubbed his chin.

Grant smiled to himself. He'd seen the look in his friend's eyes before.

"Something bothered me about the way they carried out the theft of the Superstealth," Oz said. "I've got a feeling we might be able to locate the aircraft another way if they did run out of fuel somewhere en route. Becky, can you get a map of Europe on this screen and plot co-ordinates on it?"

"No problem," she answered.

Antoine Goethals turned on the water in the lavatory of the gas station and bathed his face. He felt hot and anxious and had to keep reminding himself to calm down. Before leaving the restroom, he quickly smoked a hand-rolled cigarette containing mint leaves and phencyclidine, although he knew he shouldn't have. He adjusted his tie and went back into the sunlit day and climbed into the front seat of the lead vehicle, a turquoise Mercedes.

Like Goethals, the three other men in the car wore suits and, to a causal observer, would have appeared to be executives on a business trip. Tailing the Mercedes was a decrepit fuel truck bearing the logo of a Spanish oil company, Petroleo Internacional. The jet fuel it carried was easily mistaken for regular gasoline, making the truck a perfect cover for transporting the liquid into France. Two men rode in the tanker truck; the one on the passenger side had a rifle hidden under his seat.

They drove on without incident, though Goethals continued to fidget as the PCP took effect. The ex-con was losing his nerve and grew more and more anxious as they neared the French/Belgian border.

The Mercedes topped a hill and was waved through the Belgian check point. Ahead of them, down in the grass-covered valley, was the red and white striped bar of a roadblock designed to detain those wishing to enter France. The border patrol needed to check their passports.

"Let's not stop," Goethals suggested.

"Don't be crazy," Ferstenberg growled from the back seat. "Have you been smoking angel dust again?"

Goethals said nothing, fear rising in his throat as he eyed the weapons the three border guards carried.

"Take it easy, Goethals," the driver, Relitas, warned. Relitas pulled the car over so the customs official wouldn't have to walk far. "They're just being extra cautious because of the recent terrorist bombings in Italy. They're not going to give us a second look if you stay calm."

Goethals tried to light a cigarette as they slowed to a stop. His hands shook so badly he couldn't even strike the match. He wadded up the cigarette and threw it, the whole package, and the book of matches onto the floor of the car. His eyes became riveted on the border guard approaching the side door of the vehicle.

"Bonjour," the guard said in a tired voice as Relitas pushed the button that lowered the electric window of the car door.

"Bonjour," Relitas answered, flashing a toothy grin.

The official had an old MAT-49 submachine gun slung over his shoulder. "Passeports, s'il vous plaît," he said, leaning toward the driver. As he bent forward, the guard grasped the MAT-49 by its pistol grip to keep it from scraping against the Mercedes's hard-waxed surface.

In his paranoid fog, Goethals misinterpreted the action and went berserk. He whipped out the .357 Magnum revolver he'd concealed under the car seat, lifted it, and fired point blank into the surprised guard's face.

The explosion of the revolver startled everyone in the car. Relitas sat blood-splattered and stupefied behind the wheel, the barrel of the gun only inches from his nose.

Goethals began waving the gun wildly. "Go!" he roared at Relitas, beating on the driver's arm. "Go, you fool!"

The other two French border guards had sprung into action the moment Goethals had produced the revolver. Before he fired, both guards had their fingers in the trigger guards of their Ruger AMD rifles. A forward flick of their trigger fingers released the automatic weapons' safeties and a rearward crush of the trigger made the rifles bark in three-round cadences.

The guards' weapons peppered the car with 5.56mm bullets only moments after their comrade fell backward from the vehicle with a gaping bullet hole in his right cheek. Glass fragments and bullets splashed the four men in the car, bullets piercing arms and torsos.

A bullet fragment ricochetted from the door

frame of the car, cutting into Goethals's spine and killing him instantly. Another projectile slashed into Relitas's scalp, knocking him unconscious. He fell forward, causing the car horn to continuously drone under the noise of the gunfire.

The two criminals in the back seat of the car struggled to get down as the bullets cut into them. Ferstenberg managed to grasp the JAR-98 rifle that had been hidden on the floor in front of him. But in the tight confines of the car, he was able to get off only one quick shot before another flurry of shooting from the border guards killed him and severely injured the man next to him.

The guards quickly reloaded their rifles, watching the four motionless men for any sign of resistance. The horn of the car continued to wail as the two guards cautiously approached the car. The inside of the vehicle looked like a slaughterhouse.

In the fuel truck behind the car, the henchman riding in the passenger seat leaped from his vehicle, his JAR-98 at the ready. The two border guards approaching the Mercedes were unaware of the impending attack from behind.

The man took careful aim and fired his rifle. The caseless cartridges cycled through his JAR-98 in five-round bursts so fast they sounded like cloth ripping. The supersonic 4.47mm projectiles streaming from the gun's barrel caught the two border guards. Both jerked spasmodically with the multiple impacts, then dropped where they had stood.

The gunman bolted forward to stand over first one and then the other guard, firing a salvo of projectiles into the head of each. The gunman then opened the door of the Mercedes and fired bursts into the men lying in the car as well.

Satisfied that both the border guards and the wounded team members in the car were dead, the gunman turned and jogged back to the gasoline truck. He unlatched the door and pushed his smoking rifle under the seat. Then he jumped in and slammed the door and yelled, "Il faut se dépêcher!"

The petrol truck roared off down the highway.

CHAPTER

12

Becky hit a button that erased the screen on the System/6000 workstation and then typed in her commands. A detailed map of France and the surrounding countries appeared, major cities and highways clearly delineated on the monitor.

"All right," she said, turning to Oz, "what do you have for me in the way of coordinates?"

"Let me run my reasoning by you two first," Oz said to her and Grant. "Let's suppose the pilot of the Superstealth didn't realize we'd be able to follow him after he took off."

"He assumed the tail section was functioning," Grant said. "So he figured there was no way he'd be spotted either visually or on radar."

"Then it'd make no sense not to take a straight path to wherever they were headed," Becky reasoned.

"But what about the fact they didn't have enough fuel?" Grant asked.

"In that case," Oz replied, "they'd have headed for a source of fuel rather than their final destination. But we'd still have some idea of where they were headed before running out of fuel, *if* they'd assumed they couldn't be followed because they were invisible."

"That makes sense," Grant nodded.

"Let's plot it out and see what we get," Becky suggested.

"The catch to plotting it out is that the directional bearings we took when we followed them were pretty wide." Oz unconsciously rubbed the back of his neck. "Our compass bearings were between 42 and 48 degrees as we left Paris."

"Let's create a cone encompassing those angles and see what we get," Becky said. She paused to think a moment, then punched in the coordinates on the computer keyboard. The map seemed to drop until Paris was at the lower left of the large screen, with a cone extending from the French capital into Belgium at the upper right of the monitor.

Oz examined the highlighted area extending from Paris. It stretched northeastward through Nanteuil, Pierrefonds, Soissons, Laon, Crépy, Crécy, Marle, and Hirson to the French/Belgian border. Across the border the line went on along Chimay, Couvin, Rosee and finally entended into Liège. The pilot's attention was drawn to Liège. "There are several arms factories located in Liège, aren't there?"

"Yes," Grant answered. "They make everything from small arms to jets. If there's a market for a stolen plane within this radius, it's likely to be in Liège."

"That's *if* they were headed that way in the first place," Oz said.

"Let's assume for a moment that they were."

Grant leaned forward to squint at the map. "Can you zero in on Liège and maybe get a list of arms manufacturers there who actually make jets?"

Becky typed in several commands.

A list of three arms manufacturers appeared on the screen. Grant studied the names. "I'd bet on Jouniaux Internationale," he said immediately. "It was created after World War II and is still run more or less as a private company under the iron hand of E.E. Jouniaux."

Becky retrieved the company file and studied it on the screen for a second. "They don't seem to have any problems with the law," she remarked.

"They've just never been caught," Grant said. "I should have thought of them before, but they're like an alley cat. Everyone knows they're up to no good but nobody can catch them at it. They're always just this side of the law, and their competitors have a way of meeting with unexpected problems."

"They also entered into the fighter jet business two years ago." Oz pointed to the screen. "Jouniaux bought the tooling for the *Vampir* attack jet from Armee Universal AG at Osnabruck, Germany. And if you think about it, that'd be the perfect mainframe to build a Superstealth around."

"Look at that," Becky said, pointing to the screen. "They bought out Armee Universal after the chairman of the board met with an unexpected heart attack."

"Another of those coincidences," Grant asserted. "And then they apparently moved the plant to Liège."

Becky leaned back in her chair. "The authorities have quit looking for the Superstealth here in France. Are you going to contact the Belgian authorities?''

Grant thought a moment. ''That'd be the logical thing to do. But old man Jouniaux has connections behind the scenes. There's no telling who might be on his payroll. Just one phone call to him and he'd stash the plane out of sight or, if it didn't make it to Liège because of fuel problems, he could reroute it to another location. I think we'd better work outside of channels on this one.''

''Let's go at this from a different angle,'' Oz suggested. ''If they ran out of fuel, they might not be at Liège yet. Suppose we search along the path from Paris to Liège. How much fuel did the rep from Osbourn-Norton think they had when they escaped?''

''Not much,'' Grant answered. ''He was certain they couldn't have gone over a hundred miles.''

Becky tapped the keyboard, bringing back the map showing Paris and the route to Liège. ''So they'd still be inside France.''

''Looks like it,'' Grant agreed.

''Our two backup Night Stalker teams and the contingency of Delta Force troops are still en route for Heidelberg,'' Oz said, checking his watch. ''But we could take our chopper out and search along this line on the off-chance something might turn up. The rest of the Night Stalkers could join us when they get to Germany and their helicopters are assembled.''

''I'll have to nix that,'' Grant said. ''The Frenchies haven't agreed to let the Night Stalkers and

Delta troops do more than cool their heels here in France. I know they won't agree to having us hotshot around their country in a military helicopter. Let's rent a civilian chopper and go 'sightseeing.' They won't be able to gripe about that."

"It'd be a one in a million chance we'd see anything," Oz said, "but it's better than doing nothing. Maybe we can at least eliminate a few spots."

"And it beats sitting twiddling our thumbs waiting for something to break," Grant agreed. "Let me get an outside phone line."

Becky handed him a headset and punched one of the buttons on her desk to get an outside line.

Grant spoke quickly in French, then hung up. "It's set. Come on, Oz, let's head for the airport. Owe you one, Becky," he called back.

"More than one," Becky laughed. "Good luck."

13

KGB agent Sergei Federov sat in the first-class section of an Ilyushin IL-86 Aeroflot jet, trying to control his fear. For reasons the Russian could not fully understand, he was never fearful on combat aircraft, whether jets or helicopters. But in 1958, his father and mother had been victims of a fatal plane crash on an Aeroflot Ilyushin IL-12 as they flew from Moscow to the Baltic, and Federov had been terrified of riding on Aeroflot commercial aircraft ever since.

The KGB agent's usual solution to quelling his fears was to drink enough vodka so that he was barely conscious. But that required that he have an aide along. Today Federov flew alone, so he compensated by securing a seat in first class where drinks would be served.

Soviet first class was a joke, he knew. It offered almost nothing extra, other than slightly wider seats. And for Federov's small frame, the wide chair was actually less comfortable than standard seats. He'd ridden first class on American planes, which did a fair job of making passengers feel special. And the

French and Italians made their first class riders feel even decadent.

But, as far as Federov could tell, Russian first class was merely a way to transfer more money from the pockets of passengers into the Aeroflot bank account.

With one exception. The vodka.

He ordered another of the lilliputian bottles from the stewardess.

"Sorry, comrade," she said cynically. "We are expecting air turbulence and won't be serving any more drinks until we reach Paris."

Federov said nothing. Instead, he closed his eyes and leaned back in the chair, painfully aware of the dreadful oval ports on either side of him. He didn't dare look through them.

As the four Kuznetsov NK-86 turbofan jets on either wing droned on, the agent tried to concentrate on what he would do if—no, *when,* he corrected himself—*when* he reached Paris and started to search for the Superstealth. The seconds ticked slowly by.

Then he started to think about the one thing that always seemed to get his mind off his fear of flying: what he would buy if someone gave him a million U.S. dollars to spend.

Federov progressed unsteadily through the covered ramp that had been extended to the hatch of the Ilyushin IL-86. But the Soviet agent quickly regained his composure and walked through customs carrying a leather flight bag.

He immediately spotted the agent sent from the Russian Embassy to meet him. Federov grimaced.

Didn't these people ever try to blend in? he wondered. The man's short hair, clean-shaven face, and cheap black suit instantly pegged him as a Soviet agent.

Federov took a roundabout route and approached the man from behind. "Are you ready to go?" he asked in Russian.

The agent jumped and then turned and recognized the man from Moscow.

The black limousine slowed to a stop on the narrow Paris street. Federov checked the address. Seventeen Oudinot Street. It was correct.

"Wait here," he ordered his bodyguard, Boris Mowinski. "You have my beeper and the tape?" he asked the brawny man.

"Da," Mowinski answered.

"If I activate the beeper, you come in and have your silenced PM ready when you enter. Anyone who looks the least bit suspicious should be considered dangerous."

"I understand."

Federov climbed from the car, thankful he hadn't drunk as much on the plane as he had wanted to. He squinted in the sunlight at his watch and walked briskly along the narrow sidewalk. He climbed the three steps leading to the diminutive porch of the decrepit, three-story brick house.

The bearded giant who peered out studied the Soviet agent for a moment. "Monsieur Federov?"

"Oui," Federov answered. The giant stepped back to admit the visitor. When Federov entered, the hallway suddenly darkened with the closing of the front door.

The giant carelessly frisked the agent, missing the CZ-75 which Federov had hidden in a pancake holster at the small of his back. "This way," the behemoth pointed. He pulled an ornately carved sliding door aside on its squeaking runners.

Behind the door was a large dining room that— unlike the exterior of the house and the hallway—exuded elegance and expense. The Soviet entered.

The room had a twenty-foot ceiling, ringed with baroque plasterwork. A cluster of Regency armchairs were placed on either side of a fireplace; on the mantel, a marble bust of Julius Caesar presided.

An oak table, heavy with floral carvings, rested in the middle of the room bedecked with crystal goblets and silver trays of fruit. A pot-bellied American who had been sitting at the table rose as the agent entered and walked toward him.

"Mr. Federov, I am Calvin Smith," the man said, placing a limp hand in Federov's. Smith had long hair and a drooping mustache. Federov noted the man's bloodshot eyes, half hidden by the tinted lenses of his wire-rimmed glasses.

"These are my associates, Mr. Jones," Smith said, beckoning toward a dark-skinned, crew-cut man sitting at the table. Jones didn't rise. His skin had an unwashed appearance and he glared toward Federov without speaking.

"And Ms. Wong," Smith motioned to the black-haired woman at the end of the table.

"Mr. Federov," she said in a husky voice. A wisp of a smile crossed her thin lips and vanished, making the hard gleam in her eyes the dominant feature of her face.

"That will be all," Smith told the giant servant who waited patiently in the doorway behind Federov. The man nodded and slid the door shut as he backed out of the room.

"I hope you don't mind if we converse in English," Smith told Federov. "Have some fruit?"

"Thank you, no. I ate on the plane."

"Let's get down to business," Smith said, pulling back a chair at the table for Federov.

The KGB agent unbuttoned his jacket as he sat down and eyed Jones, who glared at him for no apparent reason. The Soviet agent decided to ignore him; he spoke to Smith. "Gavrilovich Arms is interested in dealing with you for information concerning the Superstealth."

"Well, that's great," Smith said, carefully peeling an apple with a paring knife. "But you need to remember that the price has gone up substantially. We've gone to a great deal of trouble to steal the plane."

"I have no doubt of that," Federov replied. "We will agree to pay. But my instructions are that I must actually see the plane before we make any deals. I know that won't be easy, but it is a condition that must be met."

"That isn't practical," Jones said in a gravelly tone. "You'll purchase the plans and spec sheets that we take from the plane."

"I don't know," Ms. Wong said. "Perhaps in a week or two, we could arrange something."

"But we'd need money up front," Smith added.

"I don't have that long," Federov said. "My people are concerned that the plane will be found by the authorities before we have a chance to obtain information. You must try to arrange for me to see it today or tomorrow."

"Mighty anxious, aren't you," Smith drawled, spearing a peach with the knife. "Perhaps we should give you a couple of days to think about it. Why don't you come back day after tomorrow."

"No, I need to see the plane within twenty-four hours."

Smith glanced at Wong, who made a motion with her hand.

"Mr. Federov," Smith said, rising to his feet, "I'm afraid we'll have to call the deal off. If you can't wait, then we're not interested in doing business. We have many potential customers who'll pay good money for the Superstealth specs, and they aren't trying to push us around."

"As you wish," Federov conceded, pressing the electronic signaling device in his pocket. The Soviet agent stood, sweeping his jacket to one side and grasping the butt of the pistol with his hand. "Please sit," he ordered Smith and Jones, covering them with the CZ-75.

Jones made a grab under his jacket. Federov fired across the table twice, both shots hitting the man in the face before he could extract the Walther P5 from its shoulder holster.

There was a violent splintering of wood in the hallway. A silenced Makarov pistol echoed in the hall. Federov stepped back so he could cover both the doorway and Smith and Wong. He was relieved to see his burly Soviet bodyguard crash into the dining room.

"Are you safe?" Boris Mowinski asked in Russian.

"Da," Federov said. "Did you take care of the servent?"

Mowinski nodded.

"Good. Secure Ms. Wong for me," he motioned toward her with his pistol. "Use the cloth tape. Tie her arms and legs securely to the chair."

In moments, Wong was bound to the arms of her chair, glaring across the table at the Russian agent.

"Good," Federov said. "Now get rid of Mr. Smith here. Take him to the hallway. Then see that I'm not disturbed."

Mowinski shoved Smith out the door. Moments later, there was another muffled shot from the silenced pistol.

The woman bound to the chair said, "You will never get the whereabouts of the plane from me."

Federov said nothing. He reached into his jacket pocket and removed a thin pouch containing six hypodermic syringes, each full of a clear liquid. He carefully removed the cover from one of the needles and prepared to inject its contents.

"You will talk," the Soviet assured her. With that, he shoved the needle into her arm.

14

E.E. Jouniaux put down the file and wiped the chalk dust from the partially completed firing pin. He took a deep breath, his flat belly extending only slightly. He pulled the safety glasses from in front of his bloodshot eyes so he could study the point of the firing pin as he rotated it between his fingers.

A few more strokes will even up the right side, he told himself.

Whenever Jouniaux got frustrated, the arms manufacturer returned to his humble beginnings as a gunsmith. The workers bustling about him in the weapons plant knew better than to bother their boss while he was laboring at the workbench; the firing of one man who had dared to speak years ago had taught Jouniaux's employees an important lesson.

Metal working was Jouniaux's true love; there were challenges in the job, but no surprises as there could be when dealing with foreign customers or military buyers, who had a habit of changing weapons requirements at the last moment.

Steel could be formed and altered according to Jouniaux's will. It could be checkered or made as smooth as glass. He could harden it so a file wouldn't cut it or make it soft and malleable. It could be blued as dark as obsidian or left its natural silver hue. It could become a life-giving surgical instrument or a weapon of destruction, according to his whims.

Over the last five years, working with metal had become a passion Jouniaux could seldom indulge in; as his company grew, making him a billionaire in just a decade, more and more of his time was devoted to paperwork. But today he had time to kill and a worry to forget.

So Jouniaux continued creating parts for the experimental gun he had conjured up in his mind almost a year earlier. He lowered his safety glasses and remounted the firing pin in the leather-padded vise jaws. He stroked the pin several more times with a fine-toothed file, then became aware of the figure standing silently next to the workbench.

"What?" the inventor asked in French as he again remembered the failure of his men to bring the Superstealth to his plant in Liège, Belgium. "Do you have any news?"

Leo Waeytens tugged at his lower lip as he always did when he was nervous. The childhood habit made his lip jut from his teeth. His hands were as graceful as a surgeon's and looked totally out of place on his corpulent body.

"So are you going to tell me the news or make me guess?" Jouniaux asked, angrily slapping the file into the rack behind the workbench.

"Our second team has got the fuel to the plane. But they ran into some trouble at a roadblock. The men in the lead car were killed and the place is covered with police."

"But there's a good chance we might get it," Jouniaux said, smiling for the first time in days. He took off the smock he wore and tossed it onto the workbench. The inventor turned and headed for his office, limping from the childhood wound he'd received at the hands of a Nazi SS officer.

As he hobbled along, he passed a long assembly table where three workmen put the finishing touches on the Mitrailleuse a Gaz machine guns the company was manufacturing for Indonesia. One of the men saluted as Jouniaux passed.

Jouniaux nodded at the man and continued the trek toward his office. "More cutting oil," he told the workman overseeing a computerized milling machine. It used a carbide blade to rapidly carve a block of steel into a machine gun receiver.

Jouniaux walked on, speaking loudly to Waeytens so his voice would carry over the noise of the miller. "Get ready to fit the plane with weapons when it comes in. We don't want to have problems transferring it to its home base. Is the nuclear fuel ready?"

"Yes, sir."

"Good." The inventor nodded. "Be sure to report that some of our JAR-98 rifles and ammunition were stolen. Some of them will be turning up with the car we lost at the roadblock. Have our new missiles ready to mount on the plane . . . And be sure to pay our promised bonuses if they are successful in bringing the plane to us."

Waeytens waited nervously while Jouniaux

paused to inspect a trigger from a conveyer belt. Satisfied, he laid the part back onto the belt carrying the triggers toward a parkerizing vat.

"Do we have a man standing by to repair its cloaking circuits?" Jouniaux asked as the two neared his office.

"Yes, sir. We do."

"That will be all then."

The new plane will be the crowning glory of the new missile systems we're producing, the inventor thought to himself as he entered his chrome and glass office. With a little luck, Jouniaux Internationale would become the most successful arms manufacturer in the world.

15

"Ready?" Oz asked over the small headset.

Grant tapped his seat belt to be sure it was fastened in. "Ready."

They had filed their flight plans and were cleared for takeoff. Oz started the Allison T63-A-5A turboshaft engine of the Hughes 500. The McDonnell Douglas machine brought back memories of the olive green Hughes 369 observation helicopter that he had occasionally flown in Vietnam.

The egg-shaped choppers were built for the U.S. Army from 1965 to 1970 and were generally know as "Loaches." Smaller than the Hughey, the Loach was capable of handling a wide variety of jobs from observation to ferrying VIPs or doing gunship duties with a 7.62mm Minigun or X75 grenade launcher attached to the short pylons that could be mounted on it.

Unlike the Loach, the Hughes 500 had five, rather than four, rotor blades and a T-shaped tail. The design change made the civilian helicopter slightly more stable in flight and considerably quieter, too.

The rotors whipped around as Oz started the turbine. The engine belched a thin cloud of blue smoke and then ran smoothly, quickly picking up speed. He glanced over the simple control panel to be sure the chopper was functioning properly and lifted the helicopter into the air.

Hours later, Oz and Grant had crisscrossed the French countryside over the area they had plotted as the probable route taken by the Superstealth toward Belgium. After refueling, they resumed their search, which both men were beginning to think was a waste of time.

"Let's try for another hour," Grant said. "Then let's head in and call it a day. I'm bushed."

Oz knew how the CIA agent felt. He, too, was exhausted. His mind wandered, gazing down at the rolling farmland below them as they flew northeast past the small city of Marle.

"What's that at eleven o'clock?" Grant asked, pointing forward to the left of the 500's nose.

Oz focused his attention. At the end of a patchwork of oat and barley fields was a small grove of apple trees. To the left of the grove was a clearing with a tiny farmhouse and dairy barn. The pilot pulled the chopper into a wide circle, dropping to get a closer look at the farm.

The Americans passed over the small cottage where a rusty Citroen sat parked in front. The shadow of the helicopter chased across the farmhouse as they passed. Oz slowed and dropped the helicopter lower toward the huge limestone barn behind the cottage; dairy cattle standing in the muddy barnyard stared up at the circling helicopter.

"The Superstealth would fit into a barn like that," Grant said as he inspected the crumbling structure with the binoculars he carried around his neck. "But I don't see any opening large enough to accommodate it. I suppose it would be possible to—"

"This is Home Plate calling American Two," the radio interrupted.

"That us?" Oz asked, his fatigued mind unable to recall the code name they'd adopted before leaving CIA headquarters.

"Right," Grant chuckled. "That's Becky. I recognize her voice."

"This is American Two. Over," Oz radioed back. He raised the helicopter away from the farm and headed northward.

"I've got a couple of items you might be interested in," Becky replied. "There was a raid on the Zeus III nuclear reactor near Dover this morning. They stole plutonium fuel. Enough to build several bombs."

"A possibility," Grant said. "What else have you got? Over."

"I'm not so sure about this second one. But a group tried to run through a French roadblock on the line we plotted earlier. Three guards were killed and a carload of unidentified gunmen as well. The kicker's that the guards at the Belgian checkpoint saw the gun battle even though they were too far away to help the French guards. They saw a fuel truck leaving the scene, headed into France. The authorities haven't been able to locate the truck yet. Over."

"If the Superstealth ran out of fuel somewhere," Grant said, "then they'd be trying to get more fuel to it. Do you know where this incident occured, Becky? Over."

"At the border crossing between Chimay and Hirson," she answered.

Grant quickly consulted the map. "We're southwest of there now. We'll head for the border crossing. In the meantime, contact the French authorities and let them know there might be some connection between the theft of the Superstealth and the border incident. Maybe that will make them more interested in helping us with our search for the plane. Over."

"Will do," Becky answered. "The French are pretty upset about this. I have the feeling they'll be more than willing to help us now and maybe even put some manpower into the area to help in your search. Over."

"Good," Grant said. "In the meantime, collect all you can on the Zeus III attack in case there's some connection. We'll be in touch if anything turns up. American Two over and out."

Oz pushed the control lever forward and raced for the French-Belgian border.

Within twenty-five minutes, they were circling the area, which was ablaze with the flashing blue lights of French police cars. The pilot set down the Hughes 500 on its twin skids, landing a short distance from the roadway.

As the two Americans climbed out of the chopper, a plainclothes French inspector walked toward them. "No reporters," he said in perfect English. He motioned with his hands as if he were trying to shoo them back into the helicopter.

"We're not reporters," Grant said, handing the inspector an identification card.

"CIA?" the inspector read. "We were just alerted that you might be getting involved."

"We have reason to believe what happened here may be connected to the theft of the Super-stealth," Grant said.

The inspector nodded. "We will be glad to answer any questions. And you may have unlimited access to the area," he offered.

"That isn't necessary," Grant said. "Our main concern is locating the fuel truck that was spotted leaving the scene."

"Ah," the inspector nodded. "The guards at the Belgian checkpoint say the truck went south, toward Hirson. But after that, it is anyone's guess. We have three different trucks sighted in the area."

"Three?" Grant asked, squinting in the bright sunlight.

"Oui. The orange and white Petroleo Internacional trucks are quite common. Two trucks were bound for La Capelle and the other for St. Michel. We have one of the drivers at La Capelle in custody. We should have both the others located within the hour; a bulletin has been issued to detain them."

"The truck headed for St. Michel is probably the one we're after," Oz said to Grant, recalling that the small town was located within the search grid between Paris and Liège.

"We'll see if we can locate the truck from the air," Grant told the inspector as the agent and Oz turned back toward the aircraft. "Thanks for your help," he called. "We'll contact your people if we have any luck."

"There it is!" Oz announced over the intercom. He pulled the helicopter around so that they circled the orange and white Petroleo Internacional truck which sat in front of a large grain elevator. A heavy hose stretched from the truck into the dark interior of the old building. "Any bets what they're refueling inside that barn?"

Grant studied the area below with his binoculars for a moment. "Yeah, that's got to be it. The plane would just barely fit into it."

Oz toggled on the radio, "This is American Two calling Home Plate. American Two calling—"

He was interrupted by Grant's warning. "They're firing at us."

A swarm of tracers hissed by, narrowly missing the nose of the helicopter.

Oz jerked reflexively on the collective pitch lever. At the same time he threw the control column to the right in an effort to avoid the deadly stream of projectiles.

A second man on the ground opened up with his automatic rifle. His aim was more accurate; bullets impacted on the helicopter's fuselage as it climbed higher, swinging to the south.

The aircraft was transfixed by the deadly fire for only a second, then the gunner lost his target. His bullets slashed harmlessly past the helicopter, riding on red tracer tails.

The shooting ceased as the gunners both opened their weapons to reload. They hurriedly removed new packs of 300-round containers from their belts, then dropped the packs into the buttstock of each JAR-98. They prepared to fire again.

The helicopter continued to climb as Oz fought to get distance between himself and the men on the ground. Two trails of tracers flashed far ahead of the chopper, then quickly slashed back, crossing the Hughes 500.

The hail of fire only hit the helicopter for a fraction of a second before passing behind the chopper. But during that moment, eight bullets cut into the vehicle. Two bullets crashed through the cabin, cutting holes in the front plexiglass windscreen as they exited. Others thumped into the transmission and fuselage of the helicopter.

Oz triggered the radio on again. "Mayday, mayday," he radioed. There was no answer; he tried again. "This is Hughes 500 at—"

"Save your breath," Grant told the pilot. "Our radio's bought it. Look."

Oz glanced at the radio as another barrage of tracers flashed past. A large hole had been punched into the radio's front panel; a thin column of smoke rose from the interior of the module.

A warning light blinked on. "That's not the worst of it," Oz said as he eyed the narrow console between him and Grant. "We're losing transmission fluid. We're not going to be able stay up much longer."

Another stream of tracers cut past the chopper as the pilot continued to vector and climb away from the farm below, trying to get out of range of the deadly rifles.

16

"What's going on?" Stakem shouted, jumping from the wing of the Superstealth and sprinting to the doorway of the grain elevator.

"We've got a helicopter nosing around," Hauschild growled, dashing into the dark interior of the building as he cradled a JAR-98 rifle in his arm. "I think we hit it but it'll radio for help for sure. We need to get out of here."

"Volland," Stakem yelled. "Are our tanks full?"

"Just topped," came a voice from inside the high-tech jet.

"Get the plane ready for take off," Stakem ordered his co-pilot.

Hauschild stormed toward the fuel truck. "Get your truck clear of the doorway," he ordered Poncelet, the truck driver who stood at the fuel pump in the rear of the vehicle.

"Right away," Poncelet agreed. He ran to the front of the truck, jumped in, and started its engine, gunning the vehicle forward and away from the grain elevator's doorway. He then leaped out of the truck and helped Laminne, his partner, remove the heavy rubber hose that stretched behind the truck.

"We need to come with you," Laminne informed Stakem, clapping the dirt off his hands and then hitching up the rifle he had slung across his back. "They'll catch us for sure if we stay with the truck."

"We've only got room for one of you," Stakem answered, walking behind Hauschild.

"But you've got to do something," Laminne protested.

"Laminne, you can stay with the truck," Hauschild commanded.

"Now wait a minute," Laminne warned, taking a step toward Hauschild and starting to unsling the rifle across his back. "I've kept my end of the—"

His voice was cut short by the explosion of the JAR-98. The trucker dropped to his knees, eyes wide in disbelief. Hauschild fired again; blood spattered into the air as the bullets impacted in Laminne's chest. The man dropped onto his face, obviously dead.

Hauschild turned toward Poncelet.

"Now hold on!" the trucker cried.

The killer triggered a burst at Poncelet before he could turn and run. Blood splashed onto Stakem's flight boots as he watched the cold-blooded violence with horror.

There was an abrupt silence, leaving the smell of burnt powder and blood in the air. Stakem was stunned. He turned from the shattered bodies and tried not to vomit.

"That takes care of that problem," Hauschild

proclaimed. "You'll be okay, Stakem. Come on, let's get out of here before this place's swarming with police." He clapped the pilot on the shoulder.

Stakem reluctantly climbed into the cockpit after Hauschild. The pilot reached up and released the lock on the canopy, then pulled it down, sealing the three men in the darkness that was relieved only by the dim red emergency lights. The pilot settled into his seat, put on his helmet, and buckled his harness.

"We're ready for takeoff," Volland said over the intercom.

Stakem flipped switches on his console, starting the engines of the Superstealth. He activated the cockpit screens which flickered to life, making the thick cockpit seem to become transparent as pictures were displayed from cameras on the skin of the plane.

"Are the cloaking circuits working?" Stakem asked as the engines' compressors revved to their full power.

"The tail section's flickering off and on again," Hauschild replied. "It's anybody's guess whether it'll cover us."

The pilot glanced at his instruments to see the status of the engines. All were registering optimum performance, so he lowered the side nozzles and diverted the jets through them. He throttled the engines, and the plane rose less than a foot off the floor of the grain elevator.

Stakem expertly balanced the plane on the columns of hot gas, nudging the controls to rotate the nozzles forward slightly. The blast of hot gas prodded the Superstealth backward toward the narrow doorway at the plane's tail.

The aircraft floated out of the building, still hanging suspended on jets of gas. The bright sunlight appeared on the screen above the pilot, making him blink. Within seconds he had the plane clear of the structure. Stakem turned the nose of the plane about, increased the engines' power, and lifted the aircraft higher. He then carefully nudged his controls so the nozzles of the jets pointed rearward. He gradually increased the Superstealth's forward momentum, slowly gaining speed so its wings would support the plane in the air and they could pick up speed.

"There's the Superstealth!" Oz exclaimed as he brought the helicopter around. The jet plane's tail was barely visible from the height the helicopter had attained.

"Where?" Grant said.

"See its tail section there to the west of the barn?" Oz pointed. "Watch the ground below it for the plane's shadow."

"Damn, it really is just about invisible." Grant was silent as he watched the tail rise into the air. "But you can see its shadow from up here looking down on it. How much longer can you keep us in the air?" Grant asked.

"That's anyone's guess," Oz told him. "Probably only a few more minutes before our transmission burns up. We've completely lost all our fluid."

"You're the pilot," Grant said. "You decide what we should do next."

"We ought to land. But we might cut them off before they get up to speed. What do you think?"

"Let's give 'em hell," Grant suggested.

Oz ignored the warning lights on the helicopter's console and circled so the Hughes 500 was between the sun and the Superstealth. Once he was positioned, Oz quickly lowered the collective pitch lever.

The helicopter plunged toward the shadow of the nearly invisible aircraft below.

"Where's that helicopter?" Stakem yelled over the intercom as he strained in his seat to see the screens around him. "It was behind us just a second ago. I thought you were watching it!"

"I was," Volland answered, glancing upward to look at the position where he'd last seen the small helicopter. "I lost it when they flew between us and the sun."

"What can they do?" Hauschild asked. "They don't have any armament or anything. Can't you lose them?"

"Once we get up speed," Stakem said as he levered his controls forward. "But I wish I knew—" He was suddenly aware of the darkness above him. The pilot stared upward to see the shadow of the Hughes 500 blocking the light of the cockpit.

Stakem jerked the control lever to the right to avoid having the helicopter drop on the cockpit. The helicopter's landing skids grazed the left wing tip of the Superstealth with a loud grinding of metal and plastic. The jet nearly tumbled.

"What're they doing?" Hauschild screamed as the Superstealth banked in a steep, slashing turn.

"Shut up!" Stakem yelled as he continued banking. "Where's that chopper?" He squinted into the bright sunlight. "There!" He saw the dark silhouette still coming after them. He jerked the plane hard to the left.

"Look out!" Volland cried.

Too late, Stakem realized that when he'd circled around to avoid colliding with the chopper, he'd also lost altitude. The grain elevator now rushed at the nose of the plane.

Stakem pulled back hard on the stick, slamming the crew backward in their seats. The left outrigger landing gear scraped the roof of the building.

Volland shouted, "We're registering damage to the—"

"Quiet!" Stakem interrupted. He continued to pull hard on the control stick, the plane's jets screaming as he revved them to power the steep climb. The pilot hit a switch that placed the view of the tail cameras onto the screen in front of him. In the center of the screen was the Hughes 500.

"That chopper's right on our tail!" Hauschild warned.

"I see him," Stakem answered as he continued to climb and accelerate. The pilot wished his plane were armed.

"We're starting to pull away," Volland shouted.

As Stakem watched, the helicopter began to lose speed and then bank away.

"They're dropping like a rock," Hauschild exalted. "Something's wrong with their chopper!"

The three crew members of the Superstealth watched as the Hughes 500 wheeled out of control, plunging toward the earth. The chopper crashed into a row of oak trees, its rotors ripping limbs as it went down.

17

"We've located the fuel truck," the French pilot reported over his radio. "There are two people lying on the ground next to it. Presumably dead."

The SA-330 Puma, which had been searching for some sign of the fuel truck after the killing of the French border guards, circled the grain elevator.

"There is no sign of anyone else in the area," the pilot said.

"Look over there." The navigator pointed toward a grove of trees. "A helicopter."

The pilot inspected the area for a moment, then spoke into the radio. "We've located the wreckage of what appears to be a small helicopter. We're going in to investigate." The French pilot steered the Puma toward the crash site.

He brought the aircraft down near the grove of oak trees. Fifteen French soldiers wearing olive-drab uniforms with blue berets jumped from the side doors of the helicopter.

Several of the troopers guarded the perimeter of the area, wielding FAMAS bullpup rifles. The others dashed toward the chopper, carrying medical and rescue equipment.

The Hughes 500 lay on its right side, its rotors bent and broken and its tail twisted to one side. One of the French soldiers rushed to the cracked windscreen and peered into the cabin.

Inside were the two occupants of the chopper, bruised and lacerated, but alive.

"The door's jammed," Oz shouted to the soldier. The pilot pointed to the side door which was over his head.

"We'll have you out in a minute," the trooper reassured the Americans. He turned to one of his comrades.

"We'll need to be careful," he said. "Fuel is leaking. One spark and this whole area will ignite."

"Let's try the side door."

He moved toward the lower side of the helicopter and reached up, grasping the landing strut. The soldier tested it to be sure it would hold his weight and then pulled himself onto the helicopter. Once on the side facing up, the soldier pulled a crowbar-like tool from the pouch at his belt. He wedged the instrument into the outer edge of the door, which had been bent and sprung by the wreck.

The tool grated along the metal. It produced no sparks, however, since it was made of aluminum. The soldier placed it at the edge of the door again and hit the end of the tool with the palm of his hand. This time the chisel-like blade was wedged between the door and its frame. Putting his weight on the tool, the soldier pushed down and the helicopter door sprang open.

Oz carefully helped Grant climb onto the seat lying beneath the open door overhead. The CIA agent gingerly ascended toward the opening and then grasped the outstretched hand of the soldier and was pulled out. Oz scrambled up the pilot's seat, then to the passenger's chair, and through the open door. In a few moments, he was standing alongside Grant while a medic checked both for injuries.

Soon the fuel dropping into the hot transmission began to burn. The two Americans and the French hastely retreated from the chopper and, within seconds, the machine exploded. A black cloud rose in the sunlight and bits of plastic and metal rained down into the oak trees.

Grant glanced at Oz with an odd expression and shook his head. "Pretty close," he said.

"I was beginning to think we'd lost you," Becky said as Grant entered the CIA computer room. "How's Oz?"

"Skinned up and tired, but otherwise fine," Grant said, taking the cup of coffee Becky handed to him. "He and his men are headed for Heidelberg to team up with the Night Stalkers detachment and the Delta Force that arrived in Germany just a little while ago. Any more information about the nuclear power plant?"

"We just received a video tape by courier from Interpol headquarters at St.-Cloud that you may want to see; it's a copy of what the security cameras shot of the attack at the Zeus III power plant."

"Was Interpol able to identify anyone on the tape?" Grant asked.

"Most of them wore gas masks," Becky replied. "There isn't any ID on the helicopter, and ballistic ID is doubtful. But one man took his mask off for a moment while the tape was rolling. We had a fair picture of him; computer enhancement cleaned it up. A search by Interpol and the CIA data banks have been able to tentatively identify the man as Leo Waeytens. He has a number of charges against him but the only one that's ever stuck was selling guns illegally; he was in prison for ten years. He's employed by Jouniaux Internationale."

"Sounds like we're on the right track," Grant said, sitting down. "What about the Big Bird?"

"The KH-13 has been diverted into an orbit that will take it over Belgium, but we don't have anything from it yet."

"I doubt that we will," Grant said. "I can't imagine these guys are going to leave the plane sitting out in the open for us to photograph from space."

"Are you going to the Belgian authorities?"

"I'll need to check with Director Maxwell. But when I talked to him this morning, he shared my fear that Jouniaux might be tipped off before his plants could be searched. So I suspect we may be going in without Belgian permission." Grant set the coffee cup down. "I better get a call through to Maxwell. See ya later."

Grant left for the communications office to secure a scrambled line and a private room. While he still didn't have the go-ahead, there was little doubt in his mind that the Night Stalkers would soon be making a secret trip to Jouniaux Internationale.

18

The Night Stalkers and Delta Troops made preparations for Operation Twilight Justice. Oz crossed the shadowy tarmac with the other soldiers and climbed into a helicopter. The seven helicopters sat on the runway belonging to the Seventh Army stationed in Heidelberg, Germany.

The choppers were parked in a row, their black and olive-drab paint blending into the darkness. The soldiers and flight crews scrambled through the doors on either side of the machines.

Oz felt bone tired.

He'd slept fitfully sitting in his MH-60K, which Death Song had piloted from Paris to Heidelberg. Once at the base, Oz had helped finalize the Night Stalkers' attack plans. Afterward he caught three more hours of sleep, lying on a couch.

As usual, Captain Warner was the mission's Air Assault Task Force Commander. The captain had flown on the same C-5A Galaxy transport plane that carried the six helicopters, the Night Stalkers air and ground crews, and the Delta Troops. They had spent long hours on the airplane during their transfer from

Fort Bragg, North Carolina, where the elite fighting groups were based, to Germany. Here the teams were joined by Oz and his crew which had flown in from Paris.

Using Oz's input—as well as that of Lieutenant James Victor, the Commander of the Delta Troops—Warner and his four-member staff labored for hours to finalize the plans for the assault on the Jouniaux Internationale complex. When the operation was finally initiated, Warner and his staff would maintain radio contact with Oz and oversee the fighting from the Main Command Post they'd improvised at the German base.

"We got lucky," Warner told Oz, Victor, and his own staff members as they sat around a small table making plans in a room at the air base. "Our KH-13 spotted this shadow," he pointed to a photo. "As you can see by this blow-up, it is undoubtedly the Superstealth. That seems to be one vulnerability of the system. If you get above it, you can see its shadow. The cameras on the lower surface of the plane actually make such a situation worse by duplicating the shadow created by the plane. The entire shadow is reproduced."

He placed another photo on the table. "Here, you can see the plane moving into this old hangar. The CIA believes the building belongs to Jouniaux, though the ownership is listed under a dummy corporation."

Oz tapped a map. "So the hangar is here, well south of the company's main complex?"

"Right," Warner answered. "One factor that's in our favor is the location of the hangar as well as the main complex. Since they work with various types of smokeless powders and explosives, the headquarters and hangar are both located well outside of Liège. That enables us to use our Quick Fix to jam radio signals and isolate them."

"How about phone lines?" Oz asked, setting a styrofoam cup of coffee on the table.

"Our intelligence shows everything is carried over this power and phone line here," Warner pointed to a large satellite photo lying in the center of the table. "If you knock this out on the way in, they'll be without power and phones. They won't be able to make outside contact."

"The plant should be empty of most of the employees since they don't work a night shift," Lieutenant Matlock, one of Warner's staff, explained.

"So we won't need to worry about shooting civilians?" Lieutenant Victor asked.

"Right," Warner nodded. "Your objective is to steal the Superstealth back. But if they offer resistance, you'll be free to answer in kind."

"How much resistance should we expect?" the Delta leader asked.

"They'll have security guards, of course," Warner said. "But the catch is that Jouniaux's got several teams of crack troops—mostly ex-French Foreign Legionnaires—that demonstrate weapons to potential buyers. Those guys are well trained and armed with Jouniaux's weapons—which are among the best in the world. As the recent attack on the Zeus III plant proved, they will be absolutely ruthless. *If* they have prepared for an attack."

"I know they manufacture all types of weapons

at the plant," Oz said. "But what kind of armament can we expect the defense to have?"

"That's the wild card," Warner acknowledged. He shuffled through the stack of papers and handed a sheet to Oz and Victor.

"As you see," Warner told Oz, "Jouniaux Internationale makes everything from small arms to guided missiles. You won't be able to outgun them if they've had time to prepare for you."

"So our only advantage will be surprise," Oz said, looking at Warner.

"Exactly," the commander agreed. "If they have the slightest hint that you're on the way, you'll be dead in the air. But even though they've been massing more of their aircraft around the plant than usual, they aren't flying patrols or anything like that. Most are on the ground. So if you enter undetected, they shouldn't have anything in the air."

"Is there a reason we can't use a Boeing E-3 Sentry during the operation?" Oz asked, knowing that having one of the airborne warning and control system jets in the air would enable them to know what Jouniaux had aloft.

"That would make the most sense tactically," Warner agreed. "Plus we have an AWACS based in Geilenkirchen. However, the problem isn't logistics but politics. If the operation is compromised, President Crane wants to be able to deny any knowledge of it. An AWACS in the air during the operation would make that too hard to do."

Everyone was quiet.

"All right," Warner said finally. "The bottom line is we have to hit them on the ground before they can counter our raid. Quick in, quick out. Now let's get down to business."

The small group spent several hours going over the detailed surveillance photos of the complex, trying to determine the best flight paths to take to the complex, and what sources could best counter both the ground and air resistance they would undoubtedly meet.

"Fuel is a problem for the MH-60Ks," Warner admitted after they'd discussed various refueling options. "I agree with Oz that we can't afford to carry external fuel tanks—you might really need your armament if you meet resistance, given the weapons E.E. Jouniaux has at his disposal."

"When we reach Liège," Oz said, "our fuel tanks will be about two thirds full. That would give us enough gas to maneuver and still get back across the Belgian/German line. At that point, we could pop up onto the radar and refuel, but head north into the Netherlands while we're still on radar. Then we could drop below the ground clutter, change our course, and return here."

"The Quick Fix and Apache gunships won't need to refuel," Lieutenant Matlock added. "The round trip is well within their capacity."

"That would put seven choppers in the attack but only four blips would head for the Netherlands," Warner said, rubbing his chin. "That should keep everyone confused enough to let the Osbourn-Norton team you'll take with you fly the plane back to Germany. Let's go with it."

After the air movement tables had been completed, Warner looked intently at Oz, Lieutenant

Victor, and his staff members. "Does anyone have any problems with any of our plans?" he asked, studying the tired faces around him. "We've got to have everything go off without a hitch, or the choppers and the Delta Team will be in deep shit on short stilts."

"The plans look good," Oz said.

Lieutenant Victor nodded and Warner's staff murmured agreement.

"Okay then." Warner stood and flexed his stiff muscles. "Operation Twilight Justice will begin at eleven hundred hours, German time. Oz and Victor, brief your men. I'll contact Washington and let them know we're set."

The two Army officers agreed, saluted sharply, and left the room.

After the briefing of his men, Oz fell asleep and dozed until sunset. Then he wolfed down a hamburger and french fries and prepared for the mission.

As he climbed into his helicopter, he wore a Kevlar vest over his nonflammable, two-piece Nomex flight suit just as the other Night Stalkers crew members did. The vest gave him added protection from any projectiles that might chance to pierce the armor around the cabin of the helicopter. The vest had a wealth of pockets which held a short-bladed knife, several spare magazines of ammunition, and a small survival pack.

On the pilot's right hip was his holstered Ruger P-85 sporting "Uncle Mike's" grips and containing an 18-round Ram-Line magazine of hollowpoint Winchester STHPs. Oz also carried a short, PK-15 5.56mm stockless submachine gun with a 45-round

Thermold magazine; he stowed the weapon in the mount behind his seat. He secured it carefully so it wouldn't shift position during any abrupt maneuvers he might be forced to make during the mission.

As the Air Mission Commander, Oz would direct the actions of the three MH-60K SOAs, two AH-64 attack helicopters, and the EH-60A Quick Fix helicopter during the mission. He would be responsible for insuring the unity of their efforts as well as those of the Delta group on the ground.

All the MH-60Ks, including the one Oz sat in, had six-barreled GE Miniguns projecting from the gunners windows on either side of the helicopters. Additional weapons were mounted on the ETS struts extending up and out from either side of the choppers. The struts on each aircraft had been modified to carry four, rather than two, weapons pods, including a twin 7.62mm machine gun assembly, a twelve-tube 2.75-inch rocket launcher, and a pair of TOW missiles capable of countering armored vehicles, jet aircraft, or helicopters.

In addition to the weapons pods, each MH-60K had a 532 counter measure dispenser. This pod was designed to defeat heat-seeking or radar missiles by dispensing chaff or flares when the MH-60K was under attack.

The two AH-64 "Apaches" under Oz's command were also heavily armed. The highly maneuverable gunships had the FLIR/laser aiming system in their noses slaved to a M230 30mm chaingun located on the underside of the chopper. When the gunner in the helicopter rotated his head, infrared beams and detectors mounted on his helmet and in the cockpit fed into a computer and servo-motor system, causing the gun and FLIR camera and gun to mimic his head movements.

The viewer for the FLIR/aiming assembly was in a small monocle that fitted to the gunner's helmet; the gunner had simply to look at a target to aim. A belt of twelve hundred 30mm cartridges fed into the chaingun's lockless bolt, giving it the ability to riddle any aircraft produced by Jouniaux Internationale.

Below the AH-64's pylons hung a quartet of weapons pods. They consisted of twenty-four ballistic 2.75-inch rockets similar to those on the MH-60K helicopters and eight Hellfire missiles that could be guided to target with a laser designator located in the FLIR assembly which was also controlled by the gunner.

The EH-60A "Quick Fix" was built on the Black Hawk chassis used for the MH-60K helicopters. It therefore resembled the MH-60Ks outwardly, except for the four pairs of dipole antennas mounted on each side of its fuselage and a retractable whip antenna on its lower side.

The pods on the Quick Fix's external stores suite were fuel tanks. These were necessitated because the EH-60A lacked the self-extending, external refueling probe that was on the MH-60Ks. In order to make the round trip to Liège and spend time in the air over the target, the chopper would need the capabilities of the external tanks.

The Quick Fix chopper had no armament, other than the small arms carried by the crew. Instead, the gunners and passenger compartments were crammed with electronic equipment consisting of the AN/ALQ-151(V)2 tactical communications intercept and a direction finding and jamming system that operated from the upper HF to mid-VHF frequency bands. The apparatus, capable of intercepting, monitoring, or jamming radio messages, was therefore able to make the chopper a decisive weapon on the battlefield, despite its lack of guns and missiles.

As the pilots checked their helicopters, the Delta Force soldiers strapped themselves into folding chairs in the passenger section of the MH-60Ks and buckled on shoulder harnesses.

The Delta troops were divided into three squads; each ten-man squad rode in one of the three MH-60Ks. Lieutenant Victor rode with the squad in Oz's helicopter.

Like the others in the Delta Force, Victor wore a black uniform, dark stocking cap, and ebony Kevlar combat vest so they would be harder to see in the darkness. The soldiers were armed with tear gas and stun grenades.

Half the troops carried M16-A2 rifles. Most of the others carried a silenced Colt carbine chambered for 9mm cartridges loaded with heavy, 147-grain subsonic bullets; these could be fired with minimal noise signature to reduce the chance of being detected. Three men in each squad carried an M203 rifle/grenade launcher or a Minimi machine gun.

One rifleman in each chopper also carried a Dragon anti-tank rocket capable of bringing down an aircraft; several others had LAW rockets packed in their integral telescoping launchers. The demolitions expert in each squad also carried a satchel charge of C4 explosives along with a time fuse and igniter. All the soldiers had combat knives and night-vision goggles; each man also had a gas mask strapped to his leg.

"Radio check," Lieutenant Victor called over the miniature headset he wore over his black stocking cap.

"Read you loud and clear," Oz answered.

"Good. Over and out."

Victor reached up and switched the radio off, removed it from his scalp, and let it rest around his neck. He replaced it with an intercom headset that O.T. had plugged into the ceiling of the chopper so the officer could communicate with Oz en route.

Soon Oz and Death Song had finished their preflight check. Oz spoke over the radio to the chopper pilots around him, "Twilight Pack, this is Twilight One. Status report."

The pilot of the AH-64 answered. "Twilight One, Twilight Two is set for takeoff, over."

The other five helicopter pilots quickly checked in. All were ready for battle.

Oz then switched his radio to the CAN frequency and contacted air traffic control to request flight clearance for the seven helicopters. After receiving the go-ahead, Oz switched back to his ABN frequency and triggered the radio switch in the control column.

"All right," Oz said. "We're cleared for takeoff. We'll use standard trail formation as per your instructions."

The engines of the helicopters started with low roars that increased in volume until the sound was almost unbearable. The two AH-64 gunships rose from the airfield, their strobe lights flashing.

Oz raised his helicopter and fell in behind the two AH-64s.

Behind him the EH-60A wheeled into formation. One after another the MH-60Ks lifted gracefully to assume their positions in the long line of Army aircraft.

The helicopters flew low in the starless night, using their TF/TA radar so they hugged the ground to avoid radar detection by German or Belgian authorities. Soon they had reached their air speed of 290 KPH, which would take them to Liège in approximately one hour.

A flurry of raindrops splashed the windscreen as Oz switched his radio to Warner's AATF command net frequency. "Twilight Monitor, Twilight One through Seven are away," he reported.

"Twilight Monitor reads you loud and clear," Warner said from his command center at the air base. "Silence, silence, silence," he commanded, informing Oz and the other helicopter crews to maintain radio silence until they reached their destination.

Then Warner had his staff relay an encrypted message to Washington that Operation Twilight Justice had begun.

CHAPTER

19

The Superstealth hovered over the ground of the concrete courtyard, drifting slowly into the huge hangar originally designed to hide experimental planes from the Allies during WWII. The site was also perfect for concealing the new plane from modern surveillance satellites or high-altitude spy planes.

Jouniaux glanced toward Waeytens as the two watched the plane land from behind the glass windows of the small, dusty office where they stood. "Are the missiles and ammunition ready?"

"Yes," Waeytens answered, nervously pulling at his lower lip. "The crew is on its way. The tanks and reactor will be refueled and the plane ready for takeoff within an hour. And our engineers think they'll be able to repair the electronics in the tail section of the jet."

"Good. Have the security personnel stay alert. It's only a matter of time before someone puts two and two together and comes to collect us. Are the Stingers ready?"

"Yes, sir," Waeytens answered.

"The Americans like to use the darkness when they attack. So be sure to post extra guards tonight."

"I will," Waeytens said. He stood a moment after Jouniaux had turned from him. Then Waeytens realized he'd been dismissed. He hurriedly left the office.

Jouniaux sat down on a rickety chair behind the dust-covered desk. He reached across the scarred surface and caressed a leather briefcase the courier had brought minutes before the Superstealth had arrived. Inside the valise was a king's ransom. Over the last two days, Jouniaux's brokers had liquidated most of the inventor's stocks and other assets. Now the industrialist wouldn't have to worry about the authorities confiscating his business or funds. Half Jouniaux's fortune was in a Swiss Bank account and—as for the other half—the inventor slapped the locking chain on the briefcase to his wrist. He would be certain the remaining portion, now in cash, negotiable bonds, and diamonds, stayed with him at all times.

He turned around and looked through the window as the three crew members climbed out of the Superstealth.

Soon, he told himself, soon, the aircraft would take him to his hideaway near Valpelline, nestled in the Alps on the Swiss-Italian border. There he'd wait until the search for the plane lost steam. Then, once he'd learned the secrets of the high-tech machine, he'd sell the technology to the highest bidder, whether foreign government or terrorist organization.

20

Sitting in the dark passenger compartment of the Hind-K as it cut through the turbulent night, Federov realized he was gambling with his career. But he also knew it was a sure bet. He was determined to find the plane before anyone else did.

As rain splattered on the armored hull of the helicopter, Federov thought about the events that had brought him to where he was.

After drugging Wong, Federov had learned that the group in Paris didn't have the Superstealth at all, nor did they know where it was. That part of the deal had been a sham. Instead, the three were acting as a front for one of the staff members of Jouniaux Internationale who had been planning to sell information on his own, using Wong, Smith, and Jones as a conduit to the Soviets. The whole affair had led to a dead end.

On a hunch, Federov decided to exploit the new computer system the KGB had recently installed. Using a mini-computer at the Soviet Embassy in Paris connected via phone to the KGB complex in Moscow, the agent was able to follow an electronic trail that enabled him to ferret out the information he needed.

The data had come from a Soviet Cosmos 2054 spy satellite. The device had been diverted into an orbit over Belgium during the previous week. The cameras in the Cosmos satellite took photos of Fabrique Nationale in an effort to unearth the particulars of the new active armor the company was creating. Technicians controlling the satellite from the ground had had a short segment of film left over.

The Jouniaux plant—a hotbed of new weapons systems over the last few years—was only five miles away. So the systems manager had ordered the remainder of the film packet to be utilized in taking shots of the newer arms complex on the off-chance something of interest might turn up. The photos had failed to cover the entire region, as the American spy photos had. And the pictures had revealed nothing of interest to Russian intelligence workers.

But they did have something of interest to Federov.

He found that workmen were constructing a massive hangar near the plant's office headquarters. This had been of little concern to Soviet intelligence officers examining the photos.

But the stories about E.E. Jouniaux were well known to Federov. To the Soviet KGB agent, it seemed likely that having the Superstealth close to his office would be just the way the Belgian industrialist would handle such an operation.

Federov contacted his office in Moscow.

Rather than let his superior know he was operating only on a hunch and risk a veto of his plan,

Federov told General Rimonov he had irrefutable evidence that the plane was hidden in the new hangar.

"How soon can you enter the plant?" Rimonov asked over the scrambled phone line.

"There isn't time for finesse," Federov answered. "I suggest you transfer your crew to Paris today. Then let our Mi-35 team here at the air show fly the jet crew and me to the plant. Since we know exactly where the plane is hidden, we can snatch it right out from under their noses."

There was a long silence at the other end of the phone line.

Then Rimonov finally spoke, "Any failure on your part, Federov, will have grave consequences."

As they neared the Jouniaux Internationale complex, Komonsky activated the infrared pulse jammer on the stern of the Hind-K's rotor pylon to reduce the possibility of a heat-seeking missile hitting the wash from the helicopter's engines. This, coupled with the chaff and flare dispensers strapped beneath the tail of the chopper, made the likelihood of being hit by missiles quite low. "Arm your weapons," the pilot ordered the gunner sitting in the forward cockpit ahead of him.

"Yes, sir," Nitschke answered. The gunner's fingers tapped two switches on the panel in front of him, arming the two AT-6 "Spiral" missiles at the wingtips on either side of the helicopter's fuselage. Then he activated the four UV-32-57 rocket pods, each of which contained 32 unguided 57mm rockets.

Finally he armed the under-nose twin-barreled 30mm cannon.

The gunner swiveled the binocular-like sighting unit that had been stowed to his right into position in front of his eyes. "Weapons armed," Nitschke announced to Komonsky.

The pilot sat in his secondary cockpit surrounded by an anti-fragmentation lining of its own. Komonsky switched his intercom to speak to Federov, who sat in the darkened passenger compartment behind him.

"Almost there," Komonsky said as the helicopter climbed a steep hill that, in the pilot's night vision goggles, still glistened from the rain. "ETA in five minutes."

"Good," Federov said. Within minutes, the KGB agent told himself, three Russians would be flying the Superstealth back to the USSR.

The two guards at the new Jouniaux hangar were thankful the rain had finally stopped. Giscold rolled down his collar and brushed the wetness from his face. Then he became vaguely aware of the thumping blades of the Hind-K.

He turned to speak to Bressard, his companion, but before he could sound a warning, the monstrous machine lifted above the twenty-foot brick wall of the complex.

Inside the Hind-K, Komonsky lifted the helicopter above the midpoint of the courtyard then centered the control column so the machine hung in position. The pilot gave the order to fire as he skillfully turned the agile chopper in a complete circle.

Nitschke launched the rockets. The missiles leaped from the UV-32 pods with brief spurts of flame. Instantly, the missiles struck, their warheads tearing through the complex around the chopper, ripping apart the brick walls and pelting the helicopter with the rubble.

Bressard was struck in the temple by shrapnel and killed instantly. Miraculously, Giscold remained uninjured after the blasts. He hunched over the pavement for a second after the firing had ceased, then jumped to his feet, his JAR-98 blazing as he ran for cover.

The bullets from the rifle glanced off the bulletproof glass of the cockpit, leaving broken glass and daubs of lead and copper.

Nitschke noted the trajectory of the tracer bullets and whipped the twin muzzles of the 30mm machine gun toward the area, watching in his FLIR scope for some sign of his antagonist.

Using the infrared viewers, Nitschke spotted the gunner as he fled into the shadows.

But the darkness did not provide sanctuary for the rifleman. Giscold remained visible in Nitschke's infrared viewer even as the guard dropped to the pavement, thinking he was hidden in the darkness. He aimed his rifle at the helicopter.

At the same instant, Nitschke fired the cannon.

The 30mm bullets, capable of defeating heavy armor, chopped into the pavement around the kneeling guard. The concrete chips and shell fragments lacerated his skin, bowling him over as he howled in pain.

The gunner quickly corrected his aim. Then a

second three-round burst of the huge projectiles cut the guard down.

The helicopter, resembling a giant dragonfly searching for its prey, hovered over the courtyard. Inside, the gunner and pilot surveyed the damage they had wrought and searched for any other threats. Then Komonsky lowered the collective pitch lever and set the gunship down in the center of the rubble-strewn courtyard.

The main cabin door on the right side of the aircraft separated, its upper segment lifting, its lower half dropping open to expose the boarding step just a foot above the ground. Flight engineer Ianinov stepped away from the hatch so Federov and the three members of the Soviet jet crew could leap from the side door of the chopper.

The four Russians sprinted for the hangar, splashing through the puddles as they cut across the pavement. Federov's eye was caught by the motion of a figure crouching next to the hangar's entrance. The AKR carbine in the Soviet agent's hands discharged and the guard fell. Federov fired another burst into the man's body. He twitched and was dead.

The Soviet pilot tried the hangar door. "It's locked," he whispered to Federov.

"Stand back," the agent ordered. He fired a short burst at the lock, ignoring the hot bullet fragments that ricochetted dangerously off the metal door.

The lock was bent and pierced by the impact of the bullets. Federov gave the barrier a brutal kick with his booted foot and the door swung.

The four Soviets stepped inside cautiously, vaguely aware of the smell of newly-set cement and paint as they looked around the cavernous, dimly-lit interior of the hanger.

Federov's mouth dropped open in astonishment.

The huge building was empty.

"Monsieur Jouniaux!" Waeytens shouted. "Wake up."

Jouniaux squinted in the bright tungsten light that had been switched on. For a moment he tried in vain to remember where he was. Then, as he sat up on the couch that was nestled in one end of the huge, dusty office, he saw the Superstealth through the plate glass window and remembered.

"What?" Jouniaux finally responded wearily.

"A silent alarm was tripped at the central complex. The guards don't answer our calls."

"Our decoy worked," the inventor nodded. He absent-mindedly checked the heavy briefcase chained to his wrist. "Is the work on the Superstealth completed?"

"Yes, the repairs to the tail were successful. The fuel and weapons are on board. We are waiting—"

"Get the air crew here immediately."

"They're on their way from upstairs."

"Good. Give me your gun."

"Pardon?"

"Your gun."

Waeytens handed his SIG P-226 to Jouniaux and the inventor stood. He checked the chamber to be sure the pistol was loaded, then jammed the weapon into his belt.

"Now get your men ready," he said. "It won't take the SOBs long to figure out where we are."

21

The light drizzle that had splattered the MH-60K finally ran its course as the Night Stalkers crossed the Meuse River. Oz switched off the wipers and let the last few droplets scatter from the windscreen.

A sliver of moon appeared from behind the clouds, casting dim shadows that were visible in the night vision goggles the air crews wore.

"We're nearing the SP," Death Song announced, moments after they'd crossed the narrow body of water.

The terrain following/terrain avoidance radar automatically dropped the choppers slightly, enabling them to skim the rolling farmland as their nap-of-the-earth flight took them closer to Liège. The device took the helicopters along the valley floor, lifted them over a hill, and then jumped a hedge of cedars that topped the rise.

Death Song checked the mission control computer display on his CRT.

"How're we doing?" Oz asked.

"Here's the starting point," Death Song answered, pointing straight ahead.

Oz glanced into the distance and, in the green and white images of his NVGs, could see the tall pesticide plant, its towers lit like smoking Christmas trees in the starry darkness.

The pilot switched on his ABN UHF channel and spoke to the other aircraft in the trail formation as they passed the pesticide plant. "There's our SP," he announced into the mike reaching from the left side of his helmet. "Keep your patterns low and tight and arm your weapons."

The helicopters followed the route above the curved road snaking below them. The path led toward the old hangar owned by Jouniaux Internationale, where American satellite surveillance had revealed the Superstealth was hidden.

Death Song finished throwing the switches that armed the MH-60K's weapons pods. "All weapons are armed," he warned. "I've given you the MG pod and rockets."

"Good," the pilot said. "O.T. and Luger, arm your Miniguns."

The two gunners acknowledged over the intercom that they had armed their weapons.

"Twilight One, this is Twilight Two," the lead AH-64 Apache ahead of Oz called.

Oz toggled the trigger on his radio. "Roger, Two."

"What're the fireworks up north?"

The pilot glanced out his window and saw the flashes to his right. They appeared to be rocket and small-arms fire. And they were in the direction of Jouniaux's main complex. He wondered what was going on.

"Ignore it for now," Oz finally said over the radio. "Concentrate on the run toward the objective."

He scrutinized the area again. All seemed quiet. Oz activated his radio. "Twilight Seven, come in," he called.

"Twilight Seven," the pilot of the Quick Fix helicopter at the tail of the formation answered.

"Patch me through to your EW engineer."

"Yes, sir," a second voice said over the radio.

"Any unusual radio traffic to the north?" Oz asked. "Over."

"No, sir. Nothing but regular stuff."

"Let me know if you get anything. Over and out."

The string of helicopters advanced up the hill and continued to hug the road below them.

"Twilight One, this is Seven. The board just lit up. Looks like several jets and helicopters. And some real heated conversations. They're scrambling. Over."

Oz swore under his breath, wondering how they'd been discovered before reaching the plant. "Military?"

"Negative," Seven radioed. "They're coming from Jouniaux's runway near the main complex."

"Take out their radios," Oz ordered, knowing that blanking the frequencies would no longer serve to alert anyone to the Night Stalkers' presence. Somehow, Jouniaux had been alerted to their presence already.

*　　*　　*

Federov stood in the empty interior of the new hangar, unaware of the American convoy of Night Stalkers helicopters racing past to the south of him, headed for the complex where the Superstealth was really hidden.

"We've been tricked," the Soviet hissed to the jet crew standing beside him. "Let's get away from here."

The four Russians dashed out of the hangar, suddenly aware of the low thunder of jets roaring toward them.

The four Soviets neared the Hind-K. Machine gun bullets from the jet diving toward them cracked past the chopper on the ground. The report of the discharge from the incoming plane arrived after the supersonic projectiles it fired bounced along the pavement with ugly whines, making a long ribbon of dust that raced toward the Soviets.

The bullets overtook the running men. Two of the air crewmen gasped as they were hit by the projectiles. They stumbled and fell as the plane screamed over them, landing face down in the puddles of the courtyard.

Federov reached the Hind-K and leaped through the open side entrance of the helicopter. The surviving air crewman behind the agent jerked the two-part hatch closed behind him as he climbed in.

The Soviet agent snatched the headset Ianinov handed to him and held the earpiece to his head as he spoke breathlessly, "We're aboard. Get out of here. It's a trap!"

22

The engineer sitting at the console inside the Quick Fix watched his CRT monitor and quickly jammed the frequencies being used by the jets and helicopters approaching the American convoy. As the enemy pilots switched to other frequencies, the engineer blanked those channels as well. In a few seconds, only the ABN and AATF command net frequencies being used by the Night Stalkers remained open.

Oz switched his radio to Warner's AATF command net frequency. "Twilight Monitor, Twilight One."

"Loud and clear, One."

"We seem to have a flock of unfriendlies joining us."

There was a pause, then Warner's voice came back. "If you want to abort, I'll let you call it."

The pilot quickly weighed his choices.

If they aborted, they might not have another chance to reach the Superstealth. But going into a hot landing zone meant added danger because the element of surprise was diminished, if not lost. Oz hesitated only a moment, then decided.

"We're going in. Over."

"We copy you, Twilight One. Good luck. Over and out."

"ACP," Death Song informed Oz as the jog in the road marked the turn they needed to execute.

"Got it," the pilot replied as he followed the two dark shapes of the AH-64s. The convoy vectored south for the last leg of the run leading to the old hangar.

"Twilight One, this is Seven," the operator of the Quick Fix called. "We've got three jets coming in low from the north. The choppers I sighted seem to be hanging around the new complex."

"Twilight Two and Three," Oz called to the two AH-64s ahead of him. "Move to secondary positions. We've got three jets low from the north."

"That's a Roger," the gunship pilot answered.

"We've got 'em," the second said.

The two gunships lifted upward so they could remain above the complex that was just five hundred yards ahead of them. There the heavily-armed aircraft would provide overwatch and security for the serial landing of the four MH-60Ks trailing them.

"Twilight Seven," Oz called. "Move to satellite position. We'll see you later."

"Roger," the pilot of the Quick Fix said as he peeled out of formation. The chopper would circle the complex, remaining below any radar that might be present and avoiding the area of conflict. It would still blot away any radio signals being used by the Jouniaux aircraft, making it impossible for them to coordinate any counterattack against the Night Stalkers.

"There's the powerline," Death Song warned Oz.

"I see it," the pilot replied. He veered the helicopter to the side with a rocking motion and hit the red button on the control column in his right hand with his little finger.

Three 2.75-inch rockets jetted out of the pod to his right, their folding fins immediately flicking for stabilization as they accelerated toward the wooden pole.

The three rockets exploded.

The pole toppled, its base shattered. The lights in the complex ahead of them went black as the powerline spit electric sparks onto the damp ground.

"RP," Death Song said.

"Lieutenant Victor," Oz contacted the Delta squad leader on the intercom, "we're going in."

"We're ready," Victor said, immediately replacing his headset with the radio and pulling on a stocking cap and night vision goggles. "Get ready!" he shouted over the engine noise to the men around him. He impatiently checked the safety on his M16 carbine as well as the knob on the Aimpoint scope mounted to the weapon.

The four helicopters dropped toward the open courtyard in front of the hangar accommodating the Superstealth.

Jouniaux nervously fingered the pistol in his belt as the emergency lights switched on, bathing the hangar in an eerie whiteness.

"It won't be long," he warned Stakem, the pilot of the Superstealth. "You and Hauschild get aboard. Volland, I need to talk to you."

Stakem and Hauschild dashed across the hangar toward the jet, leaving Volland waiting with his helmet under his arm, licking his lips nervously.

"As you know," Jouniaux begain, "I've become somewhat of an expert with a wide variety of weapons systems, Volland."

"Yes, sir. But I don't—"

"So I'll be riding in the Superstealth tonight." The inventor pulled the pistol from his belt and aimed it at the weapons control engineer. Both men froze in place and Jouniaux continued to speak, his eyes riveted on the technician. "Also, there's the matter of trying to sell information about the Superstealth to the Russians. You didn't know I knew that, did you?"

"But I—"

The inventor pulled the trigger of the SIG, hitting the surprised air crewman in the face. The 9mm bullet tore a neat hole in his forehead that spouted blood as the projectile impacted, splattering Jouniaux's white shirt with fine droplets.

The lifeless body crumpled into a pile of loose limbs.

The industrialist bent over to pick up the dead man's helmet, then quickly limped on his scarred leg toward the jet as its engines whined to life as Jouniaux settled into the weapon engineer's seat.

A loud explosion shook the hangar.

*　　*　　*

"We got it!" the pilot of Twilight Two exulted. The AH-64's Hellfire missile had caught the Jouniaux fighter jet as it approached, exploding in the intake scoop and ripping it apart in a blast that rained metal fragments across the farmland below.

The pilot of Twilight Two banked hard to the right to avoid the missiles launched by a second Jouniaux jet. The missiles glided past, traveling far beyond the helicopter and finally exploding in the air as their auto-destruct took over.

Twilight Two fired another Hellfire, as the string of MH-60Ks it was committed to protect neared the tarmac below. The missile followed the invisible laser beam that designated the target spot on the jet diving toward the helicopters.

The missile barely connected.

The wing tip of the jet ripped apart. The aircraft shuddered as the pilot tore at his stick, trying to regain control. But the jet twirled in a tight roll that carried it toward the earth, its canopy down. It scraped along the field and finally broke apart.

A third fighter jet continued to climb, eluding the Hellfire released by Twilight Three.

And then Twilight Two exploded in the air in a brilliant flash.

23

Komonsky, the pilot of the Hind-K, checked the instruments and craned his neck to the left, anticipating that another jet would make a run over the courtyard. He located the incoming fighter plane. "Second jet at nine o'clock," he warned his gunner as the helicopter lifted from the concrete.

"I see it," Nitschke answered. The gunner's fingers tapped the launch button for the AT-6 "Spiral." A missile accelerated from the left wing tip at the side of the helicopter's fuselage, its exhaust reflecting from the damp pavement as the chopper rose upward in the chill air.

The jet pilot sighted the rocket's back-blast as it was launched at him. He tore his plane out of its strafing run and lifted it away from the earth without firing at the chopper.

As the jet pilot tried to elude the rocket coming toward him, Nitschke manipulated the missile's controls, altering it with the coded radio message sent from the console to the AT-6's guidance system. The projectile adjusted its course, narrowing the space between it and the plane.

The jet pilot ejected a flare from the tail of the plane, unaware that his ploy would have no effect on the guided missile. The rocket closed the remaining space. It connected with the fleeing jet's tail, blowing its right stabilator, fin, and rudder to pieces.

The plane instantly went out of control, tumbling in a tight roll. The frantic pilot ejected but, as his plane gyrated, he left the cockpit at the wrong moment, hurtling toward the earth before his parachute could save him.

"The other jet's coming in at five o'clock," Komonsky warned.

Nitschke, sitting in the gunner's cabin in front of the pilot, scanned the sky with his night vision goggles as Komonsky turned the Hind-K clockwise to face the approaching threat.

"I see it," the gunner said, his fingers jabbing the fire button on his controls as the chopper lined up with the oncoming jet.

Another AT-6 flashed away from the Hind-K.

At the same moment, the jet launched a rocket, the flame of its exhaust lighting the nighttime sky and silhouetting the fighter plane against the dark sky.

Komonsky slammed the helicopter to the side, his finger stabbing at the flare-launch button as he wheeled, hoping the missile coming at them had heat-seeking sensors. A moment later, he released a similar parachute that dropped chaff to disrupt any type of radar guidance system which the missile might be using.

Nitschke tried to control his missile during the violent maneuvers of the helicopter, but lost his target. He abandoned control of the rocket and switched to the cannon controls, rotating the 12.5mm machine gun assembly under the nose toward the aircraft, regaining sight of it in his weapon's CRT. He fired a short blast at the plane and was satisfied to see it pull out of its attack.

The jet's rocket slashed past the Soviet helicopter, homing in on the dropping flare. It exploded behind the chopper, showering it with flak.

"I can get you a clear shot," Komonsky told his gunner as the jet streaked past with a flurry of shooting from its machine guns.

The projectiles missed the helicopter by a wide margin. The helicopter pilot rotated the nose of the chopper quickly, tracking the fleeing plane as it rose to make a tight turn.

"Let's save the AT-6s," Nitschke suggested.

"Give me control of the UV-32 pods," the pilot agreed.

The pilot took over the rocket pods of the helicopter, using the flight controls to zero onto his target. Watching the jet in his scope as it wheeled around, he caught it in his cross hairs, adjusted his aim below the speeding plane to compensate for the in-flight trajectory the fighter plane would be taking as it dropped back toward the helicopter, and fired a salvo of three rockets.

The unguided projectiles left with brief spurts of flame that continued to be visible as they shot toward the jet.

The jet's guns fired. One of the three missiles exploded in the air in front of the plane.

Nitschke held his breath as he watched the remaining pair of rockets.

The two missiles hit, tearing through the jet, ripping apart its fuselage and severing its right wing. The bullets from the jet's last burst pelted the helicopter's heavy armor. The momentum of the fighter carried it toward the Hind-K for a few seconds, then the air resistance broke the plane apart into a flaming mass that dropped toward the earth.

"Very good," Nitschke told the pilot.

Immediately the pilot whipped the chopper into a violent maneuver that threw Nitschke's helmeted head against the side of his canopy. Recovering from the sudden movement of the helicopter, the gunner saw a flare on a parachute as it dropped behind the chopper.

The gunner scanned the sky, expecting to see another jet or its incoming missile.

He saw nothing above them.

Then a slender missile raced past the helicopter, rising upward into the air to explode harmlessly above them.

"Ground rockets," the gunner said. "Where are they?"

"West of the hangar," Komonsky replied, shoving his control column to place as much distance as possible between the chopper and the building below them. He dropped another flare as he angled in a slightly different course in order to make the helicopter follow a less predictable route.

Using the infrared viewers, Nitschke spotted the small cluster of men near the hangar as they readied another shoulder-launched rocket. The helicopter gunner rotated the twin muzzles of the 30mm machine gun downward to bracket the group.

Just as his finger hit the fire button, another rocket leaped skyward. Komonsky's violent maneuver to avoid it threw off the gunner's shots. The projectiles went wild, pocking the roof of the hangar behind the men.

The slender missile the guards had launched raced skyward toward the helicopter. The pilot altered his course again, releasing another flare from the tail of the Hind-K.

Nitschke watched the missile which seemed to come right at the chopper, but at the last fraction of a second, the infrared pulse jammer on the side of the helicopter disrupted its guidance system. The rocket veered toward the flare and exploded behind the Hind-K, rocking it with a thunderclap.

Again looking through his infrared sight, Nitschke bracketed the men next to the hangar. As he watched, they readied a third shoulder-launched rocket. The Soviet gunner hit the fire button as one of the guards raised the rocket tube toward the helicopter.

The 30mm bullets from the helicopter snapped through the air. They sliced into the five men and pounded craters into the pavement around them. The shattered launch tube whirled into the air from the lifeless hands of the man holding it. Then the warhead inside the launcher exploded, sending shrapnel through the bodies of the men falling around it and leaving a blackened patch on the side of the hangar.

*   *   *

After distancing itself from the hangar, Komonsky dropped the Hind-K toward the earth, hugging the farmland racing below them to avoid radar detection. The pilot set the helicopter on a southwest heading, back toward Paris.

"What happened?" Komonsky asked over the intercom.

"A trap," Federov answered irritably. "The plane wasn't even there."

"Look's like a huge firefight west of us," Komonsky remarked.

Federov turned toward the square port beside his seat. In the distance, several kilometers away, he saw a giant fire ball reaching into the sky; burning wreckage was evident on the ground as well.

Federov almost immediately realized what he was witnessing. "Take us closer," he ordered. "Avoid getting into the crossfire, but get us over there."

Oz landed his chopper as the AH-64 exploded, its fiery debris casting shadows as the fragments dropped behind the hangar.

"They're firing SAMs!" O.T. warned over the intercom. "At nine o'clock. Along the wall. I've got 'em."

The gunner jabbed the triggers of his spade-gripped Minigun. The six barrels of the machine gun rotated in a blur as it fired strings of ten rounds each time O.T. mashed the trigger. The hot casings and belt links spewed from the chute beneath the gun, dropping onto the dark tarmac as the Delta Troops jumped from the door behind the gunner.

As O.T. initiated his salvo, Oz radioed a warning to the remaining AH-64. "SAMs along the wall south of us."

Jouniaux's men raised a JSM-92B, readying the portable air-defense missile to fire at the remaining AH-64 after bringing down its sister chopper. The guard holding the missile was sheltered from O.T.'s fire as he shouldered the weapon and started to track the gunship.

"I see the bastards," Twilight Three radioed as he leveled his machine. As fire streamed from O.T.'s Minigun, the pilot wheeled his AH-64 around, dropping to avoid the shoulder-launched missile that streaked past him, leaving a dim cloud of smoke behind it.

O.T.'s salvo chewed into the concrete wall again, finding a soft spot that shattered, chopping five men and demolishing one of the shoulder-launched missiles the group carried. Then O.T. discontinued firing so the Delta Troops passing across the dark courtyard wouldn't be endangered. He glanced toward the passenger compartment.

"All the dogs're off," Luger called to Oz.

As O.T. watched, the Delta Troops raced forward toward the hangar, shooting toward the wall to the south from which came sporadic small-arms fire. One of the American combatants stumbled and fell as a bullet tore through his shoulder. He was scooped up by his fellow soldiers as the men raced toward the hangar, firing their weapons as they advanced.

There was a fiery blast from the 30mm chaingun below the nose of the AH-64 Apache as it dove toward the tarmac, strafing the Jouniaux guards who still hid behind the wall lining the courtyard.

The 30mm projectiles demolished the wall, pelting the guards with sharp concrete chips and shell fragments. Three of the men dropped without a sound. The four still able to stand scattered into the darkness.

Rockets hissed through the darkness from the pod of the AH-64. The 2.75-inch rockets left fiery slashes in the night, their explosions ripping into the earth around the fleeing men, killing the remainder of the group.

"Twilight One is taking off," Oz warned as he lifted his helicopter upward. He guided it forward, hovering over the Delta Troops as they advanced. The pilot spotted a party of riflemen wearing the distinctive Jouniaux guard uniforms. They fired a .50-caliber machine gun mounted on a small jeep approaching the hangar. Their deadly crossfire cut down several Delta Troops who were readying a satchel charge at the heavy doors of the hangar.

Oz kicked a pedal on the chopper and dipped the MH-60's nose slightly as he thumbed the button on the control column. The machine-gun pod to his left blazed.

The bullets from the weapons pod caught the jeep, pocking its windshield, ripping into the men inside the vehicle. The jeep came to a halt, its gun firing a brief flurry as the dead machine gunner's hand gripped the weapon's trigger for a final moment.

From the right of the chopper, Luger's Minigun spit a salvo toward an approaching van full of guards firing from its side door. The bullets from Luger's gun chewed into the engine of the vehicle, then climbed over the cab and into the passenger compartment as the vehicle sped toward the airstrip. Luger fired a final burst and the vehicle suddenly swerved and rolled to a stop, its occupants dead or dying.

Another long blur of flame spit from O.T.'s Minigun as he spotted a second van approaching from the west. A fusillade of 7.62mm bullets chopped into the windscreen of the vehicle. The van raced out of control until it crashed into the first van in a maelstrom of metal and glass.

Flames erupted overhead, rocking the courtyard with a violent explosion.

Oz rotated his chopper and glanced at the flash that lit the sky.

Above and north, the AH-64 Apache tumbled across the sky.

"Fighter coming in low from the east," one of the chopper pilots on the ground warned over the radio net.

The fighter jet which had hit the helicopter with one of its missiles continued its run, barely discernible to Oz's eyes as it raced toward the airfield. The jet's cannon blazed, strafing Twilight Four and Five as they sat on the ground.

One of the MH-60Ks exploded as the incendiary bullets ignited its fuel tanks. The other remained in place, seemingly unscathed.

Oz shifted his helicopter to the right as the jet passed, a second volley from its cannon sending bullets cutting through the air where the MH-60K had been moments before. Oz coolly swung his chopper around to line its FLIR on the tail of the fleeing jet. The American pilot pushed the control column hard forward so they accelerated to diminish the rate at which the aircraft sped away from them.

Oz tapped the button on the control column with his little finger. The 2.75-inch rockets on the pod to his right hissed away from the helicopter on tails of flame, chasing the jet as it continued to outdistance the chopper.

The pilot of the jet pulled his stick hard to the side, dogging the missiles chasing him. The rockets raced past, one missing the aircraft by only meters.

"Ready with the TOW," Death Song informed Oz as the pilot adjusted their course so they remained on the jet's tail.

"Take him," the pilot ordered.

Death Song concentrated on the high resolution VID screen in front of him as he fired the guided rocket. The projectile exploded from its tube in the pod on his left. He adjusted its flight with the two joysticks he held, their electrical signals coursing through the wire that uncoiled from the rocket.

The jet banked, preparing for another run at the field, nearly completing its turn as the warhead sliced into its fuselage. There was a small explosion but the plane continued on for three seconds as if nothing had happened.

Then the rear of the plane disintegrated as its fuel tank exploded with a brilliant flash, the rubble arching forward for some distance due to the speed the plane had attained. As the helicopter crew watched, the burning wreckage tumbled through the sky to be lost from sight behind a hill.

Moments later, secondary explosions of the plane's armament rocked the night.

Oz slowed the MH-60K and rotated the machine back toward the hangar where the Superstealth waited.

The engines of the high-tech plane powered up inside the old hangar as the battle raged outside. The noise cancellation circuits left only a loud hiss.

"Open the hangar door," Jouniaux told Waeytens over the radio.

Waeytens, who stood ahead of the plane, signaled one of his men as he yelled to those around him. "Get ready!"

The guard tripped the switch controlling the large hangar door. The six men inside the hangar prepared their JAR-98s as the massive door cracked open and swiftly lifted on its motorized rollers.

The large aperture splashed light across the courtyard, illuminating the five Delta Troops who had been preparing to blow the door open with their C4 explosives. One of the Americans dropped the satchel charge. The others raised their rifles toward the guards who knelt with their weapons pointed at the soldiers.

Both groups fired at nearly the same instant.

In the resulting melee, both the Delta Troops and guards were discharging their weapons at near point-blank ranges, the massive salvos quickly downing all but three of the Delta Troops.

All of the guards were killed except for Waey-tens.

One of the soldiers fired another three-round burst at Waeytens as he struggled to bring his JAR-98 up to shoot again. The henchman dropped on his face, the life torn from him with the impact of the deadly blast.

The American soldiers turned their fire toward the Superstealth as other American troops rushed in from either side of the hangar to join them.

"Go," Jouniaux ordered as the American rifle bullets thumped against the Kevlar surface of the plane, wrecking several cameras which made black holes in the view screens lining the canopy.

The plane lifted into the air, hovering a few feet from the floor of the hangar, inching ominously toward the soldiers who continued to fire.

"Switch off the noise cancellation circuits," Jouniaux shouted to Hauschild.

The electronic countermeasures engineer flicked switches.

An overwhelming whine and thunder filled the hangar.

The soldiers standing inside the entrance in front of the jet dropped their weapons and fell to their knees, holding their hands over their ears as the deafening roar was reflected off the back walls of the hangar to engulf them with its cacophony.

Only one of the soldiers ignored his pain. He yelled in torment, his voice lost in the tumult as he shouldered a LAW rocket. He aimed at the source of his agony and his fingers removed the weapon's safety and then stretched toward the fire lever.

Jouniaux trained the machine gun encased in the turret below the cockpit on the man. He thumbed the firing button as the lever on the LAW dropped.

The long, withering barrage clipped the soldier holding the LAW as the rocket erupted from its launch tube. But the flaming projectile went wide of the mark, blowing a hole in the back of the hangar as the trooper fell dead.

The industrialist fired again at those on their knees with their hands clamped over their ears, cutting them to bloody tatters. Then he discharged a third salvo at the soldiers running across the tarmac in the distance.

The bullets chattered, and broken concrete plumed around the soldiers, cutting three of the men down as they sprinted. The others scattered, eluding the lethal fusillade.

Jouniaux paused as the Superstealth cleared the hangar, then centered his gun on one of the MH-60Ks still on the tarmac. When the chopper was in his sights, he again thumbed the trigger.

The helicopter's pilot frantically tried to raise the chopper from the runway as the bullets danced across the MH-60K. The volley penetrated the windscreen and tore into the pilot and co-pilot. The helicopter lifted into the air abruptly as the pilot spasmodically yanked the collective pitch lever in his left hand.

After reaching an altitude of sixty feet, the chopper wheeled out of control into the blackness of the night. It lost altitude, scraping along the roof of the hangar and then tumbled off the structure's far end.

The chopper's blades whipped apart against the concrete as its engine continued to throb.

The Delta Troops who had regrouped again fired their weapons at the Superstealth as it rose into the air. Its underside reflected the flames of the burning vehicles. Oz raced toward the high-tech plane, his machine guns silent since the Delta Troops might have been caught in his fire.

As the pilot watched helplessly, the Superstealth winked out of sight as its cloaking circuits were activated.

24

"I can still see its shadow!" Death Song exclaimed.

Oz circled to get in line directly behind the accelerating Superstealth. He matched the speed of the jet as he triggered his radio. "Twilight Monitor, this is Twilight One."

"This is Twilight Monitor," Warner answered. "What's your status? Over."

"We've run into stiff resistance," Oz said. "Both Apaches are destroyed. All the rest except ours and the Quick Fix are severely damaged. We're in pursuit of our objective. But it could out-distance us at any moment."

"You know your orders," Warner answered.

"That's a roger, over and out," Oz replied. He knew he was to destroy the high-tech jet if they couldn't retrieve it in order to avoid having it remain in the wrong hands.

"We've got a jet coming up fast from four o'clock," Stakem said. "And a helicopter on our tail."

"Is the jet ours?" Jouniaux asked.

"I can't tell if either is ours, since they've got the radio jammed to hell," the pilot answered.

"Doesn't matter," the inventor said. "Go east and lose them. They can't stay with us for long."

The pilot eased the stick to the left, banking the Superstealth into an eastward heading.

"They're following us," Stakem warned after checking his instruments. "And the jet's going to just miss intersecting our course!"

"Our cloaking is engaged, isn't it?" Jouniaux asked Hauschild.

"Affirmative," the electric countermeasures officer answered, looking at the green board in front of him, which also had a few yellow lights interspersed in its patter. "We have a few cameras knocked out. Probably from small arms fire. But not enough to matter much from any distance."

Jouniaux watched his aiming scope as he rotated the 30mm machine gun to face the helicopter following them.

Death Song scrutinized the penumbra of the Superstealth as the plane flashed over the rolling farmland. "I can just barely make out where it is," the co-pilot told Oz. "Sort of a shimmering in the moonlight above its shadow."

"Can you target it?"

"I think so."

"Let's use your second TOW, then," the pilot ordered as he changed his course slightly to continue to follow the jet.

"Twilight One, Twilight Seven," the Quick Fix called. "We've been getting traces from two TF/TA radars. A jet's coming toward you low and from the south at high speed. And we had a helicopter that got lost in the ground clutter. Looked like a Soviet, but I don't know how that's possible."

"Thanks, Seven," Oz answered. "We're going to concentrate on the prime objective first, then we'll deal with the jet and any other chopper. Keep us posted."

"Roger."

Death Song again jerked the TOW controls and view screen toward himself. "Hold it steady," he told Oz.

Oz kept the helicopter on course, matching the speed of the nearly imperceptible Superstealth ahead of them.

Death Song launched the TOW. The rocket hissed forward in the darkness, its trail etched for a second into the NVG Oz wore.

"Twilight One, that jet's almost on top of you!" the EW officer in the Quick Fix called on the ABN net. "Still accelerating. I'm sure it's one of Jouniaux's."

"Keep it steady," Oz whispered to Death Song over the intercom, hoping the message didn't distract his co-pilot. Oz looked to his right and could barely see the aircraft which appeared to be on a collision course with the Superstealth.

A large flare sparked from the launch tube at the tail of the Superstealth; but since the TOW was not a heat-seeking missile, the distraction had no effect on the rocket gaining on its target.

Death Song's eyes were riveted on the high resolution VID screen in front of him. Using the joysticks, the Native American adjusted the flight of the missile through electronic signals conveyed along the wire that spooled behind the rocket.

A moment before the missile reached its target, the jet approaching at right angles to the helicopter fired a salvo of rockets. The projectiles passed harmlessly past the helicopter and failed to sever the wire controlling the TOW. But then the approaching aircraft flew between the chopper and the Superstealth.

Oz watched in dismay as the jet exploded in front of them, its wreckage scattering in the darkness.

Death Song swore as the MH-60K flew through the thick cloud of smoke left behind by the plane.

Oz aligned the helicopter with the mirror-like Superstealth and hit the fire button on the control column with his little finger. The hi-tech jet started to accelerate and climb, releasing a flare at the same instant Oz fired. The helicopter's rockets passed harmlessly beneath it as the aircraft released another flare.

As the Superstealth leaped upward, its shadow on the ground became smaller. Oz watched the shimmering area of the sky, matching its climb. There was a small flame under the nose of the hi-tech jet.

A loud thump sounded on the side of the MH-60K and metal detectors lit on the console.

"They're firing at us!" Oz said, realizing that the flame he'd seen was from the muzzle of the jet's gun.

The shimmering pattern in the sky ahead of them shifted again and then Oz lost it. He studied the sky for a few seconds and then spoke on the intercom to his co-pilot. "Do you see it?"

Death Song scanned the sky, trying to pinpoint the fleeting image again. "No! It was there and then I lost it when it banked."

Oz continued to climb, hoping the gunner in the Superstealth would be tempted to fire at them again and give away the jet's position. As he lifted the chopper, he switched to the ABN net and toggled on his radio, "This is Twilight One. Is anyone besides Twilight Seven online?"

"That's a Roger. This is Twilight Five."

"What's the status on the ground there?" Oz asked.

"We're still able to fly but the rest of the choppers in the party are totaled. The troops have the field secured. Fifteen dead and twenty stretcher cases. Some of the remainder are walking wounded."

Oz continued to watch the sky as he spoke into the radio. "Okay. We're heading back. Load the wounded into your chopper and head for the refueling point. Don't wait for us. Have the troops secure some vehicles, if possible, and head for their emergency point A to await dust-off later. I'll come in to ferry the dead. We'll—"

"High at eleven o'clock," Death Song interrupted.

"Hang on, Twilight Five," Oz said. He studied the sky and saw a shimmering distortion sliding across the heavens, altering the position of the stars ever so slightly as it moved.

The pilot clicked the radio on again. "Twilight Five, have Twilight Delta take the best means to point A along with the dead. You take the wounded to your refueling point. We will not, repeat, will not be returning to you. We are again in pursuit. Over and out."

As Oz switched to Warner's radio frequency, a burst flashed at the tail of the Superstealth.

"They're firing at us," Oz warned as he shoved the control column to the right, pushing downward on the collective pitch lever so the chopper dropped. The crew hung nearly weightless in their straps as most of the projectiles flashed overhead, one skimming the roof of the chopper.

There was a second burst of light.

A moment later, one of the projectiles slashed into the cabin of the MH-60K.

25

Oz threw the chopper into a dive as the last of the projectiles crashed through the cabin of the helicopter. The ground rushed toward the nose of the aircraft.

The pilot yanked on the collective pitch lever, the change in speed causing the helicopter to shudder, and the heavy G forces flattened the crew into their bucket seats.

Oz leveled the chopper out and held it steady. Then he spoke over the intercom. "Everyone all right?"

"Okay back here," O.T. answered.

The pilot glanced over at his co-pilot, who had his helmet off. Death Song rubbed the top of his head, signaled a thumbs up and flashed one of his rare smiles. The helmet he had been wearing sat in his lap, crumpled nearly in two by the projectile that had come through the windscreen in front of him, leaving a gaping hole in the plexiglass.

"O.T.," Oz said. "Can you bring a headset forward for Death Song?"

"Will do."

A few seconds later, O.T. leaned between the two seats in the cockpit and traded the co-pilot a headset for the ravaged helmet.

"Damn," O.T. said, examining it as he retreated back into the gunners cabin, "were you wearing this when it got hit?"

"Sure was," Death Song said over the new headset. "And I have one hell of a headache."

"It's a wonder you still have a head to ache!" Luger said from the back.

"All right," Oz said. "Let's stay alert. I still have the Superstealth. And it seems to have lost us in the ground clutter, though they'll probably sight us again before long."

"Where is it?" Death Song asked as he replaced his NVGs.

"Ahead at one o'clock. Seems to be changing its course."

"I've got it," Death Song said.

"Any damage you can see back there, O.T.?" Oz asked.

"I've been looking around," O.T. reported. "We've got a hole in the floor behind Death Song. And it looks like the outside right door's got a long crease where one of the Superstealth's bullets clipped us. But I don't see any major damage."

"Good," Oz said. The panel in front of him showed metal fragments but all the sensors showed the engine and transmission in good shape.

Better call Warner, the pilot thought to himself. He glanced at the frequency setting then triggered the radio on his control system, "Twilight Monitor, this is Twilight One. Come in please."

There was no answer.

"Twilight Monitor, come in please."

Then the pilot realized there wasn't any static on the radio. There was no sound at all. "Death Song, do you see anything wrong with the radio?" he asked.

The co-pilot inspected the AN/ASC-15B tri-service radio module and C-6533/ARC radio on the panel located between him and the pilot. The equipment looked functional. Death Song tapped it with his fingertips. "Do you suppose it was damaged by the gunfire?"

Oz tried again with no results, then swore. He switched to several other frequencies, listening intently and hearing only a pop or click as he worked the selector. "Deader than a hammer," he finally announced, hitting the module with his fist.

The pilot glanced ahead at the Superstealth and again adjusted to stay behind it, then studied the vertical situation display on the CRT in front of him to check their direction.

"We're headed southeast now," he told Death Song.

"We were going east last time we contacted any of our group," the co-pilot said.

"Right. Warner will have no idea of our present location, since they've slowly changed course since our last radio message."

Death Song spoke, "And if we break off with the Superstealth to connect via phone from a house on the ground—"

"We'll lose them," Oz finished. "Our only

chance is to stay with the Superstealth. What've we got in armament?''

"Both TOWs are gone," Death Song answered as he glanced at his board. "You've got five rockets and who knows how much ammunition in your MG pod."

"Not much," Oz gauged.

"I've got about a hundred rounds here in my Minigun," O.T. said from the back.

"Mine's just about exhausted," Luger said. "Maybe twenty or thirty cartridges at the most."

"How about heading up and getting onto the radar?" Death Song asked. "The Belgian authorities would scramble a jet."

"But our friends in front of us would probably pick us up first," Oz protested. "If they didn't nail us, the jets would order us to land. And they'd miss seeing the Superstealth to boot."

"Just like Paris," Death Song agreed bitterly.

Oz punched up the fuel and power management on his HSD screen and studied it a moment. "We have, what? Maybe fifteen more minutes in the air."

"Yeah," Death Song answered. "A little more if they keep their speed down to 260 clicks per hour."

The pilot was silent for a moment, and then spoke. "Okay, here's what we'll do. We'll keep sharp and hope they get to where they're headed before we're treading air. If not, we'll have to try to take them with the little armament we have left. I just wish we had more fuel so we could tag them. They don't seem to be able to see well enough to locate us back here."

"I have an idea," O.T. called from the back.

The pilot smiled. O.T. usually had an idea. But more than once his ideas had pulled them out of tight spots. "All right, let's hear it."

Everyone listened as O.T. explained his scheme.

"I think you got 'em with that last volley, Mr. Jouniaux," Stakem said. "That chopper dropped like a rock. I sure can't see them in the screen. And there's no radar or infrared signature."

"There wouldn't be any infrared," Jouniaux said. "They've pretty well got that covered in the Black Hawk choppers. And they could avoid the radar by keeping close to the ground. Damn the cameras in this plane!" he cursed angrily. "They're just not sharp enough to really see what's outside!"

The industrialist fiddled with the contrast of the display in front of him that showed what was behind the plane. He twisted a knob to boost the picture, enlarging it until it was too grainy to see any details at all. Finally he gave up in frustration.

"I think we lost them," Hauschild tried to reassure him. "I watched the monitor when you fired. You had them dead on."

Jouniaux shook his head, "I still feel uneasy. Too bad they weren't where we could use our missiles on them."

The cockpit was silent for a moment and then the industrialist spoke again. "How long before we reach Valpelline?"

Stakem checked his vertical situation display

and then his FPM before answering. "About two hours, more or less."

"Can't you go any faster?"

"Yes. But there's a catch. If we go much beyond 280 kilometers per hour, the noise cancellation gets erratic. Anybody on the ground could hear us. If the authorities questioned enough people, they could plot our route and eventually discover—"

"All right then," Jouniaux snapped, rubbing his stiff leg. "Let's stick with the quietest speed. But stay sharp."

After the battle between the American convoy and the Jouniaux jets had finally come to an end, the Soviets had tagged behind the Superstealth and MH-60K, maintaining a safe distance as they headed eastward.

"I see it!" Nitschke shouted excitedly from the dark forward cockpit of the Hind-K as it hurtled through the night, hugging the earth to stay hidden from the high-tech jet as well as the American chopper.

"Where?" Komonsky asked, squinting behind the night vision goggles he wore over his face.

"The Superstealth is far ahead of the American chopper," Nietzke pointed. "They're about where that bright star is. I saw their guns when they fired at the helicopter."

The pilot studied the spot, and then saw the shimmering in the sky ahead of them. He whistled quietly. "No wonder everyone is interested in stealing that machine!"

26

"The Americans are landing," Komonsky informed Federov over the intercom.

The Soviet agent was startled by the sound of the pilot's voice and realized he had fallen asleep. "Are you sure?" he asked wearily.

"For some time they've been veering off to check the roads," the pilot answered.

"Now they've swerved and are dropping into the trees," Nitschke added.

"But why would they be stopping?" Federov asked. "Is the Superstealth still—"

"It's still ahead of us," Komonsky answered. "No sign that it's landing."

"Then why are they stopping here?" Federov mused.

The pilot studied the crude map on the computerized screen in front of him. "We're west of Beho and east of Saint Vith," he said. "Just a couple of little towns near the Belgian/German/Luxembourg border. Nothing here of interest as far as I can see."

"Fuel," Nitschke conjectured. "The Americans have exhausted their fuel. They're carrying weapons pods on their pylons. Without their external fuel tanks, the U.S. choppers can't go far.''

"Of course,'' Komonsky agreed.

"How's *our* fuel?'' Federov asked, suddenly worried about something he'd given no thought to before.

"We have an hour's worth left in our tanks.''

"And the Superstealth?''

"It's hard to say,'' Komonsky answered. "But if they had time to fuel it before they left, they could go on for many more hours. The plane is designed for long-range bombing runs and—''

"If they haven't reached their destination in an hour,'' Federov interrupted, "is there any way for us to refuel without losing them?''

"We can't refuel in the air. But it only takes moments for us to refuel on the ground.''

"How could we do it?''

"I suggest we have fuel airlifted and deposited on the route we seem to be taking. They haven't deviated at all from 171 degrees since we started following them.''

"Is airlifting fuel possible on such short notice?''

"As slow as we're traveling, our tankers could drop fuel bladders off. There'd be a problem of airspace violation, of course. But if they came in low, I doubt that anyone—''

"Connect me to Moscow,'' Federov ordered. "And stay on the line so you can give them the coordinates we'll be passing across.''

O.T.'s idea was deceptively simple: land near a gasoline station and tank up the helicopter. Since the

MH-60K had been designed to operate on a wide range of fuels, this would be practical, even though it would lower the efficiency of the helicopter's engine somewhat.

In a few minutes, they'd sighted a service station on a side road.

Oz pulled the helicopter into a tight curve, dropping between the pines growing along a narrow stream, and raced toward the narrow road. He followed it back to a decrepit-looking gasoline station sitting at the outskirts of a cluster of small bungalows.

The pilot maneuvered the aircraft over the small station, thankful it didn't have a roof over its rusted fuel pumps, and set the chopper onto the broken tar surface.

"Helicopter at nine o'clock," O.T. announced over the intercom.

"I see it," Oz said, his night vision goggles enabling him to discern the helicopter as it passed. "See the projection on its nose?"

"A Soviet Hind-K," Death Song suggested.

"That's what I'd say," Oz answered. "They don't have many of those fielded. I'd be willing to bet those're our friends from the Paris Air Show. Come on, let's get refueled."

The Americans climbed out of the MH-60K, stretching stiff muscles in the cool night air as the Hind-K's thumping was lost in the distance.

"Do you suppose they've radioed the coordinates of the Superstealth to the authorities?" Luger asked as they sprinted toward the front door of the unlit filling station.

"Wouldn't put money on it," O.T. said.

Oz beat on the front door of the station that also doubled as the home of the attendant. Lights sprang on and man in a white nightshirt pushed aside the curtain and peered out. He swore loudly in German as he cracked open the door.

"Ja?" he asked.

Payment for the gasoline was made in cash and a trade. It consisted of all the cash the Night Stalkers had and O.T.'s Stock & Yale glow-in-the-dark digital watch.

The small station had a phone, but the operator who answered didn't speak English nor did any of the people in the nearby cottages—as far as the Americans could decipher from the station owner's German. So Oz left a message with the man to be delivered to the police. In it, he gave the Superstealth's course and speed.

Because of the language problem, the crew had no idea if the message would even be delivered. But there was little else that could be done. The Americans quickly climbed back into their chopper and took off.

As they crossed the border and entered Luxembourg, Oz continued to push the MH-60K at its top speed of 290 kilometers per hour. They maintained their heading of 171 degrees, flying low to avoid detection by the local government, the Superstealth, and the Soviet chopper tailing it.

The Americans soon climbed out of the farmland and into the low Ardennes mountain range that extended from Germany's Rhineland across northern Luxembourg.

Death Song was rechecking the figures he'd entered into the helicopter's mission computer. "We definitely should have overtaken them by now," he said.

"We've either missed them or they've altered their course," Oz answered. "We'll circle for a couple of minutes and hope they come through here soon. But if they've altered their course much, we've lost them."

The American chopper hugged the Clerf river valley that had cut deeply through one of the rocky hills in the squat mountain range. The pilot pulled the MH-60K in an ever widening circle as he and the other crew members kept their vigil in the darkness.

But a quarter of an hour later, the Soviet Hind-K helicopter and the Superstealth it followed were nowhere to be seen.

27

"I know there's something back there," Jouniaux
said as he played with the contrast of the CRT display
in front of him. The forest below seemed like a sea
of shadows on the monitor. But every once in a while
the industrialist could swear he saw a shape, creeping
through the murky sky. He twisted a knob to enlarge
the picture.

"There," he said loudly. "I'm sure I saw it."

"I don't see anything," Hauschild said, after relaying the impulses from Jouniaux's screen to the
one sitting in front of him.

"Bank to the right," Jouniaux ordered Stakem.
"And increase our speed. Let's see if we can lose
them or force their hand."

The pilot throttled the engine and pushed his
stick to starboard, throwing the plane into a sharp
bank.

The Superstealth passed over a black mountain
lake. As Jouniaux watched in the low-light television
camera, the Hind-K created a contrasting specter
that floated over the dark body of water.

"There it is!" Jouniaux shouted, sure now that his hunch had been right.

"There is a chopper back there," Hauschild said in dismay.

"Get in line to take them," the industrialist ordered.

As Stakem brought the plane into a tight circle, Jouniaux rotated his cannon and fired a long burst toward the oncoming helicopter.

Komonsky spotted the muzzle flashes of the Superstealth's cannon and threw the Hind-K to the side before the projectiles started ripping into its titanium armor.

"What's going on!" Federov demanded from the back after banging his head on the side of the cabin during the violent manuever.

"They've spotted us," Komonsky shouted as another burst of light appeared from the turret under the plane circling toward them. "Request permission to return their fire."

"No!" Federov replied with such force Komonsky started at the distortion in the earphones. "We must not damage it."

"Missile launch!" Nitschke warned.

Komonsky threw the Hind-K into a steep bank that nearly rammed them into the low hill of pines that came speeding toward them. He quickly released a flare and chaff, hoping one or both would confuse the homing device on the rocket.

The missile streamed toward the helicopter, ignoring the flare that had erupted from the tail of the chopper. The projectile was lost for a moment in the chaff; then it regained its bearing and headed for the fleeing chopper.

The guided missile approached the Hind-K, then raced past, missing the chopper by a wide enough margin to prevent its proximity fuse from igniting the warhead. The projectile continued in a long arc, ending in the small lake below. It made a giant gusher that broke the silence of the peaceful valley with its thunderclap.

Another volley of cannon fire rattled off the thick armor of the Hind-K as its pilot sent the chopper into another sharp turn.

"He's on our tail," Komonsky warned Federov. "He can outrun us and destroy us if we don't fight back."

Another clattering of projectiles ripped through the tail of the Hind-K as Komonsky altered his course once more.

"All right, return fire," Federov muttered reluctantly.

Nitschke didn't wait for orders from the pilot sitting behind him.

He rotated the dual machine gun in the turret below the nose of the chopper, watching the screen until he had the weapon aligned on the shimmering section of the sky where the Superstealth was hidden.

As he tapped the firing button on his gun, he saw a rocket drop into sight, materializing from the invisible bay door on the underside of the high-tech jet.

"Missile launch!" Nitschke warned as the exhaust jetted from the rear of the guided rocket.

Komonsky shoved forward on the control column, increasing the pitch of the rotor's five main blades for maximum speed. Simultaneously, he raised the collective pitch lever, lifting the Hind-K into a steep climb that threw him and his passengers backward into their seats. His fingers danced on the countermeasures buttons. Two chaff dispensers flew from the rear of the helicopter, creating a cloud of metal confetti that scattered the radar beam guiding the missile toward them.

The stubby wings on either side of the Hind-K gave it greater lift than most helicopters enjoyed. Komonsky now used this lift to full advantage in his frantic effort to escape the missile racing toward him. The chopper climbed quickly into the cold air.

"Hard left, hard left!" Nitschke screamed as he watched the oncoming missile in the FLIR of his gun turret.

Komonsky threw the control column to the left, kicking the left pedal at his feet in the same instant. The Hind-K fell into a tight circle. The pilot shoved the control column forward and depressed the collective pitch lever, causing them to drop and gain greater speed as they banked left.

The rocket hissed past to the pilot's right, coming close enough to cause two of the eight miniature laser sensors in the nose of the missile to trigger the annular proximity fuze. The warhead automatically detonated. Fragments of the casing and missile peppered the exterior of the Hind-K, and the aircraft shook as the pressure wave of the explosion reached it.

Komonsky swore in Russian as he continued his

tight circuit, bringing his chopper around to where he thought the Superstealth must be. But he couldn't locate it. "Where are they?" he shouted over the intercom, scanning the area in front of the nose of the helicopter.

"At one o'clock, high above the horizon," Nitschke said. "Permission to fire Spiral."

"Fire!" Komonsky yelled, still unable to see the aircraft.

Nitschke hit the button, watching the section of the sky nearly three miles away where the plane hung in the air, suspended on the downward blast of its jets.

The AT-6 streaked from its tube at the end of the Hind-K's wing, its four fins popping into place in a blur of motion as it reached its maximum speed. "Now it's your turn," the gunner vowed to himself as he guided the missile toward its target.

"Incoming missile," Stakem warned, pushing forward on the control stick to take them into a steep dive.

"Jam it!" Jouniaux ordered Hauschild.

The electronic countermeasures officer searched his board for the correct button to activate the electronic chatter that would confuse the missile's guidance system.

"Jam it! Jam it!" the industrialist demanded.

"All right, all right," Hauschild finally found it. He jabbed with his forefinger.

The effect was instantaneous. The missile charging toward the Super Stealth suddenly veered off to the side as the electric yammer from the plane's EW assembly jammed the control signal from the Hind-K.

"That did it!" Hauschild gloated. "Now let's take 'em."

The moment the AT-6 had veered from the Superstealth, Nitschke had realized the problem. "They're jamming it."

Komonsky was ready.

He had the helicopter lined up on the Superstealth as it continued its dive toward the forest. The Soviet smiled to himself. The pilot had been foolish to take the aircraft so close to the ground and limit his maneuverability. "Give me the UV-32's."

The gunner transferred control of the rockets to his pilot.

Komonsky fired.

Five of the rockets jetted from the torpedo-shaped pod on the Hind-K's wings. The Soviet pilot carefully spaced the launches so every avenue of escape was blocked.

The Superstealth could either crash or be hit by the rockets. There was no other alternative.

28

Far north of them, Oz spotted the blast of the warhead.

"Unless I miss my guess," the pilot drawled, "those are our friends up there."

"Must have discovered they had a Hind-K tailing them," Death Song suggested.

Oz straightened the chopper out and headed north. "Better arm the weapons, Death Song. There's no telling what might happen if they're slugging it out. We might get lucky and down the Superstealth while it's busy with the Soviets."

Jouniaux swore loudly when he recognized the trap they'd fallen into. The unguided rockets were indifferent to the electronic jamming signal the Superstealth was emitting. They dropped relentlessly toward the jet as it skimmed along the top of the forest.

Moments after the launch flash, Stakem jerked his stick first to the left, then the right in the vain hope of eluding the missiles. He had no time to even think before the rockets were on top of him.

Four of the missiles skirted the Superstealth, crashing into the timberland and exploding harmlessly.

But the fifth rocket struck the plane.

From the corner of his eye, Stakem saw the warhead bury itself in the left wing and, in just a fraction of a second, detonate.

Debris exploded from the wing, and the left flap was ripped apart. Inside, the pressure wave bent the titanium and Kevlar ribs and tore a hole in a section of the composite skin.

The plane vibrated violently. Stakem fought the control stick, keeping the plane from going into a tight spin as the instrument panel in front of him lit with damage warnings.

The pilot hit the throttle, pushing the plane to a higher speed so he could gain altitude. As the plane bucked in the air, it threatened to pirouette into the foliage just a few meters below.

Federov watched in dismay from the side window of the Hind-K as the Superstealth careened across the forest.

"We've got them now," Komonsky said jubilantly over the intercom as he turned the helicopter to follow the oscillating aircraft. "One more salvo should take them out of the air."

"No!" Federov ordered. "Cease fire and just follow them. They're already going to crash. We want the plane in one piece, if possible. Radio our position to Moscow and have them divert the tanker."

*   *   *

The Superstealth continued to shake violently as its computerized system attempted to restore stability to the controls.

"Let's eject!" Hauschild shrieked, his eyes riveted on the lower edge of the view screen. Treetops seemed to be racing only inches below them.

"Not yet," Jouniaux said evenly. "Take it easy."

As abruptly as it came, the jarring stopped as the computer compensated for the lack of flap control. The plane once again became responsive to the pilot.

Hauschild heaved a sigh of relief, but continued to grip the arms of his bucket seat.

"I seem to have control again," Stakem whispered hoarsely, surprised to even be alive. Though the pilot had been briefed by the engineers at Osbourn-Norton that the computerized controls could recover from massive damage, he had always assumed it was only so much advertising hoopla.

"Bring us around to face the helicopter," Jouniaux ordered.

"Yes, sir." Stakem complied by lowering their speed until they hung on their jets, then turned the aircraft to face the oncoming Soviet helicopter.

As the Superstealth hung on a column of hot gas, Jouniaux punched the launch control.

A guided missile dropped from the bay on the lower side of the fuselage of the hovering jet. As the missile's engine ignited, a continuous wave radar pulse sprang from the Superstealth, illuminating the Hind-K to the radome aerial inside the nose of the rocket. The sensor steered the missile toward its target, altering the hydraulically-driven delta wings at its midsection to compensate for any movements the helicopter made.

The jet crew watched as the Hind-K pilot two miles away struggled to avoid the missile that chased after him. The projectile followed the helicopter into the steep climb and compensated for the sharp turn the chopper made.

The missile was distracted by the chaff dispenser and missed the Hind-K. Then the laser sensors in the nose of the missile triggered the annual proximity fuze.

The explosion shook the nearby chopper, bending the titanium armor on its right side and fracturing the glass next to the pilot. A chunk of the metal plate ripped apart, swinging through the passenger compartment along with bits of deadly shrapnel. Smoke filled the compartment and Federov became weightless as the helicopter plunged toward the earth below.

CHAPTER

29

Federov plummeted through the darkness, half stunned by the force of the missile that had exploded ahead of him. His ears hurt and he could barely hear Nitsche's voice as the gunner struggled with the unresponsive controls of the helicopter. As they hurtled downward, their speed only dropped slightly before the jarring crash that ended with the splintering of trees and groaning of metal.

Federov sat dazed for nearly a minute in the smoke-filled darkness of the cabin. He tried to speak into the intercom, then realized his headset had fallen off. When he withdrew his hands from his head, they were sticky with blood.

The smoke grew thicker and the Soviet agent started to choke. The smoldering seat burst into flames and the light revealed the bloody bodies of the flight engineer and jet pilot.

Federov wondered if there was any danger of the fuel in the chopper igniting.

In near panic, he fumbled with the harness, his eyes stinging with smoke. He was struggling to breathe as he grappled with the latch on the side entrance of the compartment. The double doors opened and he fell out of the chopper into the darkness.

The agent lay hugging the moist earth for a few moments. Tears washed the acrid smoke from his eyes.

"Are you all right?" Nitschke asked, standing over the agent and flicking a flashlight over the man.

Federov struggled to his hands and knees. "Yes," he choked out.

Nitschke squeezed past the agent and climbed into the passenger compartment, blasting the tiny fire that burned inside with a fire extinguisher. The cabin became pitch dark and the gunner reached up and flicked on the emergency light.

The harsh red glow revealed the broken bodies of the flight engineer and the Soviet pilot who was to fly the Superstealth. The two corpses hung forward in the harnesses of their seats where they had soaked up the fury of the blast, their bodies protecting the KGB agent who had been sitting behind them.

The gunner turned away and stepped out of the aircraft into the fresh air.

Federov shakily rose to his feet. "Are they alive?"

"Both dead," Nitschke replied. "They were dead before we ever reached the ground." The gunner walked to the front of the chopper and climbed onto the two boarding steps molded into the surface of the fuselage. He reached back and tapped on the heavy glass of the pilot's side window.

Komonsky sat slumped in the cockpit, his face

lit in the ghostly light of the instrument panel. A tiny trickle of blood ran from under his helmet and down his cheek.

Getting no response from the pilot, Nitschke jumped down and ran around the front of the chopper to the right side. He climbed the boarding steps to the side door of the pilot's cockpit and gingerly unlatched it. He rotated the door out of the way on its bent, stiff hinges and reached in to the unconscious man.

The MH-60K flew over the rolling farmland of the Bon Pays region of Luxembourg.

Oz glanced toward his right. In the distance the Superstealth flew parallel to the American helicopter. The plane was no longer invisible. Its damaged wing was readily apparent against the background of stars; the cloaking circuits had obviously been damaged by the Soviet missile.

The pilot recalled the air battle. The sight of the olive green Hind-K dropping into the forest was like many of Oz's nightmares. The American felt no great love for the Russians, but he could identify with the terror of plunging toward the earth in a helicopter that failed to respond to its controls.

"Looks like they still haven't spotted us," Death Song commented, breaking Oz's reverie.

"So far so good," the pilot agreed. "We'll continue to travel parallel to them. We can maintain a safer distance that way and I suspect the sensors along that wing are damaged as well. I'm going to try our radio again."

Oz switched the mechanism on and tried several different channels. There was nothing.

"I wonder if the gasoline station attendant ever contacted anyone," Death Song said.

Oz adjusted his stiff frame in the bucket seat. "I doubt it."

"I bet he holds it until the police come through," O.T. said from the back.

"That's my bet, too," Oz agreed. "Since daylight's still several hours away, it could be four or five hours before the police get it. From there, it's anyone's guess what they'll do with it. We're on our own and could be for days."

The pilot reached over to the heating module located on the console between the two front seats and adjusted the control knob a bit farther toward "hot." "We're going to have to tag the Superstealth and hope they land before we run out of fuel," he said. "Then we can take them."

"What if they outlast us on fuel?" Death Song asked.

"Then we'll have to try to knock them out of the air."

"We ought to stand a fair chance of doing that, as crippled as they appear to be," the co-pilot said.

"Maybe. But I was amazed at how they recovered from the Soviet missile strike. I have a feeling it won't be easy to bring that bird down. I'm hoping it won't come to that."

As the gunner touched Komonsky, the pilot groaned and sat up.

"What the hell are you doing," he asked,

through tight lips. "You think I'm dead or something?"

"You all right?"

"Yes." He unbuckled his harness. "Now get out of the door so I can see how much damage there is."

"Are you sure you should get out? Maybe—"

"Get out of the way." The pilot grinned at the gunner's concern. "Don't treat me like a sick child."

As the three men inspected the Hind-K, they discovered the chopper had sustained most of the damage on its lower surface. The gun turret and FLIR/LLTV assembly, as well as the ventral sensor pack, were all bent into uselessness.

Nitschke had managed to take over the controls when Komonsky had been knocked unconscious by the blast of the nearby missile. The gunner had extended the landing gear a few seconds before their crash, which had helped to break their fall. But in the process of protecting them, the landing gear had been severely damaged; the struts were bent and the shock absorbers were leaking fluid.

"The flight controls are okay," Komonsky said after taking a quick inventory of the damage. He continued his inspection of the chopper with the small flashlight he held.

"What repairs are needed?" the KGB agent asked, recalling the depressingly long time it normally took to get anything repaired in the Soviet Air Force.

"All that's needed is to leave this panel off so it doesn't rub against the control rod linkages," the pilot answered, pointing to the area exposed by the removal of a panel from the front of the passenger compartment.

Federov studied the three titanium rods in the wall behind the pilot's cockpit. The chunk of armor thrown through the passenger compartment had bent the panel so it rubbed against the rods, making it nearly impossible for the gunner to control either the tail or main rotors during the emergency landing.

"The damage to the blades themselves is minimal," Nitschke added from behind the two men.

"Nitschke," the pilot said to his gunner, "I don't know how you managed to land us in such a small clearing."

"That," the gunner admitted, "was purely a coincidence."

"Can you get us back into the air?" Federov asked. "We have a chance of catching the Superstealth if we can get back into the air quickly."

"We should be ready by the time our fuel and paratroopers get here," Komonsky answered, rolling up the sleeves of his coveralls.

C H A P T E R

30

The Soviet chopper was refueled from the bladder tank parachuted into the forest, along with three squads of troops, from an IL-76M jet. The cargo plane's four turbofans had rocked the quiet forest as the aircraft came in low, aiming for the flares Komonsky had lit on the ground. The giant jet completed its drop and then circled to depart, skimming along the forest top to avoid radar detection.

Half an hour later, Federov was sitting in the back of the Hind-K as it hurtled through the cold night. The helicopter traveled at its top speed in an effort to catch the Superstealth, maintaining the same heading as before.

Air whistled into the passenger compartment through the hole left by the missile strike. In the cold cabin, Federov was flanked by seven Spetsnaz troops who silently endured the wintry conditions, the hoods of their jackets pulled over blue berets. Night vision goggles hung around each man's neck; all the special troops were armed with AK-74 rifles with folding metal stocks. Several of the soldiers carried short RPG-18 anti-armor rocket launchers.

As usual, Federov felt uncomfortable in the presence of the Spetsnaz troops, even though he was more than their equal in training and fighting skills. He hated their fanaticism. In more than one battle, the agent had seen the special troops take unnecessary risks and endanger the lives of those fighting beside them.

And unnecessary risks were something Federov avoided whenever possible. It was better to plan well and minimize the need to take risks in the actual conflict.

Federov's thoughts turned to his radio contact with Moscow prior to takeoff. The Soviet agent shivered—and not solely because of the cold.

General Rimonov had informed Federov in unequivocal terms that his career would be in jeopardy if the Superstealth continued to elude him.

"And be sure to retrieve any papers or luggage Jouniaux is carrying with him," the general had ordered.

"His luggage?" Federov asked.

"KGB Intelligence has discovered he liquidated most of his assets early this week. Some of the money's undoubtedly in secret bank accounts. But we believe he escaped with a huge sum of cash and other negotiables. If you retrieve those, they could be put to good use in our organization."

"I'll be sure to check," Federov had promised.

The Russian agent blew on his hands and rubbed them together in an effort to warm them. The helicopter passed out of Luxembourg and into northeastern France.

Federov closed his eyes and once again

dreamed about what he would do if he had a million American dollars of his own.

The Superstealth continued its slow progress toward Jouniaux's hideaway, crossing through France and into Switzerland. Soon the snow-covered Alps towered in the darkness far ahead of the jet.

"We're starting to lose fuel more quickly," Stakem informed the industrialist as they crossed Lake Neuchatel west of Bern.

"How can that be?" Jouniaux demanded. "I thought you said we had a *slow* leak."

"We did," Stakem said irritably. "And now I'm telling you we're losing more. The leak's enlarged. And the added wind resistance from our bum wing isn't helping any, either."

"How much longer can you keep us in the air?"

The pilot punched three buttons along the side of his STAR display and hit some keys on the computer keyboard. "Assuming the leak doesn't get much worse, we can't make it all the way to Valpelline, but I think I can get us into the Alps, at least."

"We'd stand a chance of remaining hidden if we can get into the Alps," the industrialist ruminated.

"You could get fuel brought in from your stronghold in Valpelline," Hauschild suggested. "We could refuel in the mountains and reach our destination in less than an hour."

Jouniaux nodded in agreement. "Get Valpelline on the radio," he said. "I have five helicopters there. They can transport fuel to us and form an armed escort."

31

The thin Alpine air made the blades of the MH-60K labor harder to keep the chopper airborne. And the fuel didn't provide nearly the mileage Oz had hoped for.

"Looks like it's time to try to take them out," the pilot announced to his crew as they crossed over another of the steep mountains. "Luger, O.T., you awake back there?"

"Roger, Captain," O.T. answered.

"Get your weapons ready. I'm going to go in high and behind them where they seem most vulnerable. But that jet still has a lot of firepower left in it, so stay sharp."

"The rockets and MG pod are armed," Death Song warned Oz. "You have control."

The pilot let the Superstealth pull well ahead of them, then circled to the right so the helicopter was behind the jet. Oz then lifted the MH-60K higher, taking it above the axis of the jet so it couldn't train its cannon turret on them.

Oz's finger was ready to tap the rocket-launch button on the control column.

* * *

"Another 'copter!" Hauschild cried out in alarm, scanning the display behind them.

"Where?" Jouniaux demanded.

"Behind us. My God, they're attacking!"

Although Stakem wasn't sure exactly where the helicopter was other than behind them, he throttled the engine and shoved his stick forward, taking advantage of the fact they were over the top of a peak. His action threw the plane into a long dive, increasing their speed and putting distance between them and the helicopter. He then punched his screen controls to see the image from the rear cameras.

"American Army chopper," Stakem said after catching a glimpse of the aircraft. He banked to the left in an effort to get farther from the helicopter. As he gained more speed, an alarm sounded. He glanced at the panel as he guided the plane around the slope and then slowed down.

"Why are we losing speed?" Jouniaux shrieked. "They'll catch up with us, you fool. Put some distance between us and—"

"You want to fly this thing?" Stakem interrupted belligerently. "If we go any faster, we'll come apart. The damaged wing is causing the plane to vibrate faster than the computer can compensate if we speed up. Now, I'll try to get above him so you can get a clear shot. But let me do my job."

The Superstealth passed over a frozen lake at the base of the mountain, then climbed up the next slope.

"They're still on our tail," Hauschild warned

nervously as he watched his monitor. "Missile launch!" he suddenly screamed.

Stakem threw the Superstealth into a tight bank that enabled them to travel at right angles to the rocky mountain surface, nearly skimming a granite wall that loomed in front of them.

In an effort to disrupt the missile headed toward them, Hauschild hit EW buttons that sent out pulses of energy in the infrared, radar, and radio spectrum.

The rocket streamed past the jet, shattering into the mountain with an explosion that battered the Superstealth with stones and created a small rock slide that rumbled toward the vale. A volley of machine-gun bullets pricked the armor of the jet. Then a second rocket jetted from the helicopter.

"Another missile launch!" Hauschild screamed again.

Stakem altered his course, throwing them hard to the right. They skimmed down the mountain slope with the helicopter struggling to stay behind. The rocket missed them by a wide margin and dropped into a glacier, where the explosion created a tall plume of snow and ice.

As the Superstealth started its ascent back up the butte, Jouniaux fired at the helicopter. His finger jabbed the fire button and a volley of cannon fire rattled off toward the helicopter, going wide of its mark before the industrialist had time to compensate for his aiming error.

"Get some altitude," Jouniaux ordered. "Get us faced toward him so we can use our missiles."

"He'll have us eating rockets if we slow down

and face him," Stakem growled through clenched teeth.

He brought the stick back, taking them high in a tight roll and then leveled off. But the helicopter had anticipated his maneuver and was nearly out of range. Stakem swore. "That pilot is damn good!"

"Not that good," Jouniaux barked as he stabbed the missile launch button on the console in front of him. "He's let us face him."

"Missile," Hauschild cried out.

The helicopter fired at the same moment the rocket left the Superstealth.

"Two," Hauschild bawled as another jetted away from the MH-60K.

The clatter of bullets echoed in the plane as a salvo from one of the Miniguns of the chopper hit the Superstealth, knocking out several more of the plane's miniature cameras.

Stakem again threw the plane down the slope, ignoring the warning lights that showed he was exceeding safe air speed with the damaged wing.

The first rocket raced past and exploded ahead of them. Then the second collided with the very tip of the damaged wing. The shrapnel from the explosion knocked out more of the cameras on the left side of the plane and an alarm sounded.

The jet begin to shake violently.

"They've fired a missile," Death Song warned as the rocket left the bay of the Superstealth.

Oz turned the helicopter down the mountain, following the Superstealth's course. The pilot increased the pitch of the main rotor for maximum speed and dropped the collective pitch lever so they skimmed along the rocky slope.

Death Song activated the countermeasure pod, releasing several chaff dispensers, since he knew the American missile was undoubtedly radar-controlled. The parachutes hung in the air for only a few moments since the helicopter was so close to the ground, but they succeeded in creating two clouds of metal confetti that scattered the radar beam guiding the missile toward the MH-60K.

The chopper continued to plunge down the incline.

Death Song anticipated Oz's next maneuver and released two more chaff dispensers.

The pilot lifted the collective pitch lever, shoving everyone into their seats with the sudden upward climb of the helicopter. Death Song released a final chaff dispenser as Oz took them into a long turn.

The rocket hissed past the helicopter. It exploded on down the slope as its annual proximity fuze neared the face of a rocky cliff.

Oz pulled them around so they were nearly behind the Superstealth again. He fired his dual machine guns at the jet, which seemed to be waffling out of control as it flashed down the mountainside.

"The pilot's losing it," Death Song warned as the plane neared the floor of the valley.

"Maybe," Oz said. "But I'm not taking any chances." He lined up the chopper on the plane. As it reached the valley, the helicopter pilot launched his last three 2.75-inch rockets.

The Superstealth continued to blunder about in the valley as its pilot fought to regain control.

The rockets from the American helicopter caught up with the jet. Two shot past, but the third connected, blowing a hole into the right wing of the plane, just ahead of the aileron. Debris from the wing tumbled through the air and ripped off the top edge of the tail fin.

Almost instantly, the jet regained stability.

As the Night Stalkers watched in dismay, the plane evened out and started to ascend the mountain on the other side of the valley.

Death Song swore softly, watching in disbelief.

"What happened?" Hauschild asked, still gripping the armrests of his seat.

"I'm not sure," Stakem answered shakily, studying his instrument panel. "The last missile hit the other wing. It must have evened the weight out enough for the computer to regain control and compensate for the damage. Should we counterattack?" he asked Jouniaux.

"No," the industrialist said. "Let's try to outrun them. They've undoubtedly radioed our position and we're going to have Swiss fighter jets on top of us here soon.

"Try for our rendezvous point," the inventor continued. "Once we have the support of my gunships we can deal with the fools in the helicopter if they're still with us."

"Yes, sir," Stakem said, eyeing the MH-60K that followed from several miles as the Superstealth topped another snow-covered peak.

32

"Here you are," Becky said to Grant as she approached him in the corridor of the CIA's Paris bureau, her high heels reverberating in the wide hallway.

Grant smashed out his cigar in the sand of the large ashtray. "What have you got?" he asked, taking the paper she handed him.

"I'm not sure it's on the level," the blond answered. "It just came in from Belgium."

"This is Oz's handwriting all right," the agent said, examining the faxed sheet. He glanced at his watch. "Took long enough getting to us. Come on, let's see where this would put them."

Grant leaned over the System/6000 workstation as Becky entered the information from Oz's note. She tapped a final key and the machine plotted the course on a projection of Europe.

"Assuming they maintained the same heading and speed," Grant said after studying the map, "they should be in or near Switzerland." He thought for a moment and then spoke. "Call the airport and have the Learjet ready, will you? I'll contact Washington from the plane. We don't have any time to waste."

The Superstealth raced ahead of the MH-60K until the helicopter was little more than a dot on the glacier-covered mountain slope far behind the jet.

"We're almost out of fuel," Stakem said evenly. "That last hit ruptured the fuel line in the wing. Shall I radio our position to—"

"Yes," Jouniaux interrupted as they flashed over the summit. "Land in this valley. Be prepared to get back into the air. If that chopper catches us on the ground, there'll be hell to pay."

"That's as far as we go." Oz lowered the helicopter, steadying it in the gust of wind that wailed across the snow-covered peak. He lowered the chopper to the rocky ground, throwing up a blizzard of loose snow as the dual turboshaft engines began to sputter.

The powerplant of the MH-60K wound down, leaving the helicopter in an abrupt silence that was broken only by the gusts that shook the vehicle. Sleet rattled against the skin of the aircraft and then everything was silent again in the snowy darkness outside.

"Now what?" Death Song asked.

"I guess we walk," Oz answered. "We could try to hole up here, but without food or warm clothing . . ." The pilot didn't finish his thought.

Death Song studied the horizontal situation display on the CRT in front of him. "There's a small village about six kilometers west. That stream running through the valley below us would lead us right to it."

"With any luck," Oz said, studying the electronic map, "we could walk away with just some frostbite to show for our adventure. All right, let's shut down and get going. The sooner we get started, the sooner we get there."

"It should be daylight in about forty minutes," Death Song said.

"Now if we just had some hot coffee," the pilot chuckled ruefully. He turned and yelled through the narrow opening behind him. "O.T., collect the emergency blankets and other gear."

"Yes, sir."

"Captain!" Death Song exclaimed.

"What?"

"I don't think the Superstealth climbed back up the hill. Look, isn't that it down there in the draw?" He pointed down the slope ahead of the helicopter.

"O.T.," Oz called back to the gunners compartment. "You still have your binoculars back there?"

A moment later O.T. reached forward and handed the powerful binoculars to the pilot.

Oz lowered his NVGs and lifted the binoculars to his eyes. The coated lens of the optical system made the dark snow below him look as if it were lit by moonlight.

The pilot scanned the snow and rock, then concentrated on the pine trees clustered in the grassy valley. He scrutinized the area along the stream that cut through the rocks.

"There it is," he exclaimed. "Come on, let's see if we can catch them on the ground."

*   *   *

"I think we've got the fuel leak repaired," Hauschild said, climbing back into the open canopy of the Superstealth. He threw the tools and teflon tape into the small tool case and sealed it into the storage compartment molded into the interior of the cockpit.

"It's a good thing you could fix it," Stakem said as he climbed in and pulled the cockpit shut. He blew on his cold hands. "The radio's no good in this valley. The waves can't get out, so we can't call the gunships to give them our new position. But with the leak stopped, I think we may have just enough fuel to climb to the top of this summit."

"Then we could reach the choppers and tell them where we are," Jouniaux said.

"Maybe we can kill two birds with one stone, then," Hauschild remarked, settling into his seat. "I think that damned American 'copter is sitting up there on the slope."

"Where?" Jouniaux demanded.

"Back behind us. It's just sitting there."

The industrialist punched the view from the rear of the plane onto the screen in front of him. He zoomed in on the MH-60K. The black shape contrasted sharply with the snow around it. The inventor launched into a long string of German curses.

"They landed just a few seconds ago while Stakem and I were outside," Hauschild continued. "They're sitting up there in the open like they're waiting for us to make the first move."

"I don't understand why they don't come after

us," Stakem said as he readied the jet for takeoff. "They'd have us like sitting ducks down here."

"Maybe they don't have any armament left," Hauschild suggested.

"Or they're waiting for reinforcements," Jouniaux speculated. "Either way, we need to take them out so they can't relay our position to anyone. Let's get into the air," the industrialist directed.

The Night Stalkers found climbing down the frosty slope of the peak on foot was not an easy task. The desolate mountainside was covered with loose rocks, half hidden in snow and slick with ice. From time to time a howling wind whipped the climbers' exposed skin with bits of stinging sleet. As they trudged downward, the Americans lost all sense of time and struggled only to keep from falling as they neared the pine-filled valley below.

Suddenly, Oz was aware of the distant thumping of a helicopter, its sound muffled and distorted by the wind that blew across the face of the mountain.

33

The Hind-K climbed above the rock and ice, its blades laboring in the thin Alpine air.

"There're those crazy Americans," Komonsky said as the Soviet helicopter topped the pinnacle. "That's the very same chopper we passed earlier. And it looks like they ran out of gas again." The Russian chuckled as he flew past the MH-60K.

The Soviet helicopter hurtled over the slope and then dropped in a giddy fall that took it toward the valley beyond.

"And there's the Superstealth!" Nitschke exclaimed from the gunner's cockpit at the nose of the chopper.

"Do we have permission to fire, Major Federov?" the pilot asked with considerable sarcasm.

"Yes," the agent replied.

"The jet is at a disadvantage in this valley," Komonsky said. "Its cannon is too low to fire and we have enough altitude to outmaneuver it. Give me the UV-32s," he ordered his gunner.

Nitschke conferred control of the half-full

rocket pods to the pilot of the Hind-K. "The rockets are armed," he said.

The jet in the valley below them lifted, rising on a column of gas. It wheeled and raced away as it climbed the coulee.

Komonsky adjusted his flight to compensate for the jet's new heading, turning to intersect the plane's course. "They can still accelerate quickly," the pilot muttered to himself. "But we should catch them on the peak."

The two aircraft climbed the steep gradient, the Soviet helicopter slowly gaining and maintaining its position above the jet as both ascended.

At the top of the rise, the Superstealth abruptly accelerated, going into a roll that burned the last of its fuel as it climbed. In a brief moment, the plane hung upside down above the mountains, shimmering pink and blue in the first rays of sunlight that streamed above the apex. It continued its ferris wheel circle, dropping back toward the Hind-K that turned to face it. As the jet dropped, it released a missile from its bay.

Komonsky voiced a profanity and kicked the right pedal, shoving the helicopter into a parallel path along the nearby granite face of the mountain. He continued to bank until he was high in the open air above the valley then dived toward the glen with the missile close behind.

The Soviet pilot was nearly weightless in the falling chopper as his fingers tapped the countermeasures button. Three chaff dispensers were expelled from the dispenser under the aircraft's tail. Clouds of confetti scattered behind the helicopter, deflecting the coded radar beam guiding the missile to the Hind-K.

As the rocket closed, the Soviet pilot threw the helicopter into a wide turn. The missile streaked past, smashing into the face of the rock to create an avalanche of snow and stones with its explosion.

Komonsky continued his tight circuit, bringing the chopper around and countering its fall. He was surprised to see the Superstealth racing away from the battle; the jet skimmed along the floor of the valley far below the helicopter.

The Russian pilot dived, lining up his rocket sights on the jet. Launching six of his 57mm rockets, he watched them tear through the air, leaving smoke trails as they fell. The Superstealth continued to coast, drifting above the grass-covered meadow as the Soviet rockets plummeted toward it.

For a moment the Superstealth's actions baffled the Russian pilot.

Then he realized the jet must have exhausted its fuel. So be it, he thought as the rockets reached their target; the men in the high-tech plane had time and again tried to kill him—and had nearly succeeded.

The missiles exploded.

Two of the warheads blew holes in the soft tundra of the valley. Another ripped off the jet's left wing just as its wheels touched the ground. The other three cut into the fuselage, completely severing the tail from the plane.

The American jet stumbled along the floor of the valley for a moment, then came to a halt, nose down, in the mountain meadow.

* * *

Stakem was dead.

Hauschild was breathing but unconscious.

Jouniaux rested his head on the console in front of him for a moment and then unfastened his shoulder harness. He stood on rubbery legs on a cockpit floor that was tilted forward at a steep angle. He cracked the canopy open, letting it raise on its hydraulic hinge. He climbed from the broken plane to the grass-covered earth.

The industrialist limped a few steps to a small lichen-covered boulder and sat down. He was vaguely aware of the meadow grass and mountain daisies that were starting to reflect some of the dawn's early rays. The area smelled of damp earth and burning plastic. His right arm ached and he felt sick and dizzy.

"Mr. Jouniaux?" a voice asked from the shadows.

The industrialist sprang to his feet, clutching the briefcase still chained to his wrist.

A soldier dressed in an olive green pilot's uniform, discernible in the shadows, approached the industrialist cautiously, centering his PK-15 carbine on the inventor.

"What do you want?" Jouniaux asked.

"You and this plane," Oz answered.

"Who the hell are you?" Jouniaux demanded.

"Captain Jefferson Carson, U.S. Army," Oz replied.

Jouniaux shivered slightly and leaned forward. "I would pay you if you'd let me go," he said to Oz. "One million dollars."

"I think you've lost all your bargaining chips," the American pilot said. "Now sit down and keep your hands on your lap."

The industrialist glared at Oz. Then he noted the dark silhouette of Hauschild peering over the edge of the cockpit, his JAR-98 rifle aimed at the American's back.

Jouniaux sat down, starting only slightly as a rifle discharged.

The report echoed off the mountains on either side of the valley and repeated the noise of the gunshot. Hauschild's body fell back into the cabin of the Superstealth.

Oz dropped into a crouch, his carbine held at the ready, then relaxed as he saw O.T.'s chunky form step from behind the wreckage of the Superstealth.

The warrant officer gave Oz a half salute and then cautiously climbed into the wrecked cockpit of the airplane to check for other threats.

Oz turned back to the inventor to find him grinning in the dim sunlight that filtered into the valley.

"Hear that?" he asked. "Those are my people."

Oz listened to the five helicopters as their whooping filled the valley.

34

Each of the five JI-6A gunships approaching the valley was armed with a 7.62mm chaingun on its port side and a pylon containing two guided missiles extending from its starboard. The helicopters had two crew members in the cockpit and room for five soldiers in the cramped passenger compartment.

Only two of the passenger compartments were occupied, however, both with armed men holding rifles; several of the firearms also had grenade launchers mounted below their barrels. The other three choppers ferried bladders of fuel which hung from cables strung underneath the machines.

The JI-6A helicopters invaded the mountain pass by following the twisting stream, thereby concealing their advance; the ridges muffled and distorted the noise of their engines and rotors. Two of the small helicopters swooped to the earth, allowing ten Jouniaux guards to leap to the grass.

The armed men charged the crash site of the Superstealth from the east, firing at Death Song and Luger as the Americans dashed for the little safety offered by the wrecked plane. The three helicopters laden with fuel hung back as the other two JI-6As charged toward the wreckage of the Superstealth, firing their machine guns at the four Night Stalkers hiding around it.

Those piloting the Jouniaux helicopters rightly assumed the Americans were from the MH-60K that sat on top of the mountain. They were unprepared, however, for the Hind-K which dropped downward from the opposite end of the valley.

The Soviet pilot charged forward behind the three choppers that carried the fuel bladders. He launched a barrage of 57mm rockets at the rear of the machines as they hung in the air.

Although three of the rockets the Soviet fired missed, the rest connected.

One of the helicopters exploded, igniting the fuel bladder beneath it in a fiery conflagration.

The second chopper suffered damage to its passenger compartment and main rotor; the machine smoldered as its pilot frantically tried to avoid running into the mountainside. The aircraft crashed into the valley, rupturing the bladder tank below it and bursting into an orange fireball. A billow of black smoke rose up the icy mountain wall.

The third chopper limped along the valley from the direction it had come, a cloud of smoke marking its path as it vanished around the bend.

"Two to go," Komonsky said to himself. He pushed the Hind-K forward, chasing toward the remaining choppers that were now turning to face him.

One of the JI-6As made a tight turn and dropped toward the valley floor, fleeing from the battle. The Soviet pilot ignored it once he saw it was leaving to escape the danger posed by the more powerful Hind-K.

The final Jouniaux gunship fired its machine gun at the Soviet; the bullets were deflected by the Russian aircraft's titanium armor. The Hind-K charged and, as the two choppers closed on each other, they launched their rockets.

Oz ignored the helicopter dogfight above him as he dropped to one knee beside the wreckage of the Superstealth. Another burst of bullets glanced off the side of the aircraft, splattering him with bits of plastic. This was followed by a grenade explosion, mercifully far enough behind him to present no danger.

The pilot blinked to clear his eyes of the debris. Then he spotted the flicker of movement in his peripheral vision. He whirled, pulling the trigger of his PK-15.

The guard charged the plane, his rifle raised to fire, when Oz's three-round burst struck him. Bloody holes riveted his face and he fell backwards into the grass.

"Can you crawl up here?" O.T. hissed from above Oz.

The pilot glanced up and saw his warrant officer whose meaty hand was extended toward him. Oz grabbed it and leaped, purchasing a foothold with his booted foot. O.T. lifted him over the edge of the cockpit and the two flattened themselves inside the plane as a stream of slugs stitched into the plastic and metal armor around them.

"Look at this." O.T. pointed to the panels

around them. A few of the monitors were burned out, but most of the display screens inside the cockpit were still functional, revealing the terrain around the plane. Oz spotted a guard charging toward the plane, his gun held at the ready.

The pilot waited for a moment, watching the screen.

When the man briefly glanced away from the Superstealth, the American pilot got to his feet and fired over the edge of the cockpit.

The guard brought up his weapon when he heard the first shot and started firing, the tracers from his weapon climbing into the air and cracking past Oz.

The American pilot pulled his trigger again and then dropped back into the safety of the cockpit. An answering barrage of slugs from another direction tore into the armor around him.

Oz glanced again at the view screen.

Outside the plane, the target lay face up on the sod, his chest torn open by the two .22-caliber projectiles from Oz's carbine.

O.T. watched the view screen for a moment and then rose and tapped his ACR's trigger before another guard charging the plane could shoulder his weapon. The duplex slugs from O.T.'s rifle caught the man in the chest. He sprawled onto the grass at the foot of the Superstealth.

"Where are Death Song and Luger?" Oz asked, glancing around at the sections of the view screen.

"There they are." O.T. nodded in the direction of his feet, ignoring the broken body of Hauschild, who lay under the screen.

As Oz peered at the view screen, he could see the two Americans. They were hiding behind a severed wing of the plane. Five guards were advancing on them, firing their weapons as they came to keep the Americans pinned behind the wreckage.

"On three," Oz said. "Ready?"

O.T. nodded.

On the count of three, the two American soldiers stood in the cockpit and started firing over the heads of Death Song and Luger. They didn't have time to aim. Instead, they shot by reflex, their guns lined up under their eyes so they could compensate for aiming errors. The salvo was directed toward the men on either end of the line facing the Americans.

Two of the guards fell.

Oz and O.T. ignored the hail of bullets being returned. Their fingers continued to pump the triggers of the firearms, sending a storm of three-round bursts of bullets at the remaining guards.

One more man dropped as Oz and O.T. continued to mash their triggers. Within moments, the last two were dead. All five lay in a bloody tangle of limbs.

Oz and O.T. dropped back into the safety of the cockpit as another squall of bullets rained along the side of the jet.

Oz checked his smoking carbine and saw it was empty. He turned to study the view screens around him as he pulled his P-85 pistol from its shoulder harness. Seeing nothing, he turned toward another view screen. He spied a man racing forward and dropping behind a boulder to the side of the Superstealth.

"Stay down!" Oz ordered O.T. The pilot rose

to his knees and rested his pistol on the side of the cockpit. He aimed carefully.

The guard raised his head from behind the rock to fire.

Oz's finger tightened on the trigger. A single shot rang out. A 9mm hole glistened in the guard's forehead as he fell over backward.

"See any more?" Oz asked O.T.

"I think he's the last."

Oz glanced around the area. "Where's Jouniaux?"

As the Americans stepped out of the cockpit, the two helicopters high above them launched their missiles at each other.

Komonsky reflexively turned his helicopter hard about after launching his fusillade of rockets. He released chaff dispensers as the missile from the enemy aircraft rushed toward him.

The rocket's radar signals were slightly displaced in the metallic cloud; the projectile missed hitting the helicopter directly, though it came close enough for its proximity sensors to set off the warhead. The blast ripped the left landing gear from the helicopter, and the skin on the outside of the aircraft was peppered with shrapnel.

The green pilot of the JI-6A was not so lucky.

He froze at his controls as the volley of rockets hurtled toward him. His co-pilot realized—too late—what had happened and tried to take over. The rockets connected. The pylons extending on either side of the chopper tore away in separate explosions. A third rocket smashed through the bubble windscreen of the helicopter and detonated in the cockpit. The front of the machine looked like an exploding light bulb as the plexiglass burst outward.

The fuel tank of the JI-6A didn't ignite nor was the engine damaged; instead the decapitated chopper started a long, descending circle that took it over the valley until it finally lost altitude and splashed into the rocky stream bed. There, its engine continued to run, its rotors swishing as if it were waiting to take off.

Komonsky turned his helicopter around and surveyed the carnage in the valley in front of him. Then he spoke on the intercom. "Major Federov, I can take you down now to what's left of the Superstealth."

"No, wait," the agent said from the passenger compartment. "See that man running across the meadow? At three o'clock."

The Soviet pilot looked out his side window. "The man with the brief case?"

"Yeah, let's pick him up first. Then take me to the Superstealth."

35

The industrialist lay on the ground, panting wearily after trying in vain to outrun the Hind-K that had chased him down. Federov climbed from the chopper, almost feeling sorry for the industrialist.

"Mr. Jouniaux," the Soviet agent said as he approached the prone man. "I think you have something I need."

Jouniaux glared at the Soviet, then rose to his feet, holding the attaché case so tightly his knuckles turned white. "If you let me go, I can pay you—"

"Ah, yes," the Russian interrupted, "the money from your liquidated assets. Perhaps you'd be kind enough to turn over your attaché case to me."

"No!" Jouniaux shouted.

"Give it to me or I'll kill you and cut it off your hand." Federov raised his AKR. "I'm sick of all we've gone through to catch you. Do you want to do it the easy way or the hard way?"

"Let me get the key," Jouniaux snapped.

"Don't try anything," Federov begain.

But the SIG pistol was in the industrialist's hand.

The Russian pulled the trigger on his carbine, firing a long string into Jouniaux's body to be sure the industrialist didn't have a chance to get off a single shot. The man tumbled to the ground, his white shirt soaked in blood.

The agent approached the body and kicked the gun from the lifeless hand. Then Federov placed the carbine's muzzle over the chain between the briefcase and the dead man's wrist. The agent pulled the trigger on the AKR; the bullets severed the chain.

Federov picked up the briefcase and raced back to the chopper.

"Take us to the Superstealth," he ordered Komonsky.

Oz stood in front of the wreckage of the high-tech jet, holding his P-85. The Soviet KGB agent approached, flanked by his seven Spetsnaz troops.

"That's close enough," Oz warned.

"I understand," Federov said, smiling. "But I hope you realize that we were responsible for knocking down the choppers that were after you. If it hadn't been for us . . ." He shrugged his shoulders.

"What do you want?" Oz asked.

"Just leave the plane for a few minutes. Let us take a look at the wreckage and then we'll go. We won't take anything and you can have it all back. If we wanted to harm you, we could have used our rockets. But we didn't. We don't have anything against you."

"You didn't use your rockets because you were afraid you'd further damage what's left of the plane," Oz said evenly.

"I'm desperate," Federov warned. "If I go back to Paris empty handed, I'll be disgraced and, when I return Moscow, I'll be—"

"Then don't go to Paris," Oz interrupted. "But don't expect us to help you. We have responsibilities, too."

Federov took a step back. He turned and whispered something to the Spetsnaz soldier beside him. The trooper nodded and ran back to the helicopter. Federov slowly sauntered toward the wreckage of the Superstealth, his hand snaking toward his carbine.

"I'm sure we can work something out," he said, his finger edging toward the trigger of his weapon.

Oz cautiously brought up his pistol.

O.T., Death Song, and Luger shouldered their rifles as the Spetsnaz troops lifted theirs.

"Now let's take it easy," the Soviet agent warned, aware of how vulnerable he was standing out in the open.

The thumping of distant helicopters broke the impasse.

The din grew louder as Federov stepped back. "Perhaps we will meet again someday," he said. He turned around and gave terse orders to his men. They all raced toward the Hind-K and clambered in.

Within seconds, the Soviet helicopter lifted into the air. It raced away to the north as a string of helicopters bearing the insignia of a white cross on a red background approached from the east. The ten aircraft settled around the wreckage of the Superstealth while three fighter jets raced above the valley, cracking the air with their sonic booms.

Three squads of Para-Grenadiers in red, green, and brown camouflaged uniforms leaped from the helicopters. The soldiers formed a broad ring around the wreckage of the Superstealth, their StG90 rifles held at the ready.

Oz tightened his grip on the P-85, wondering what was about to happen.

"It's okay," a familiar voice said. "The Swiss are with *me*."

"Grant," Oz grinned as he holstered his pistol.

The CIA agent ambled across the field toward them, a billow of smoke blossoming from the cheap cigar between his lips.

E P I L O G U E

Oz slept for nearly eighteen hours after the Night Stalkers returned to the U.S. He awoke to find Grant sitting by his bed.

"Thought you might be interested in this," the CIA agent said very matter-of-factly, dropping a paper on the bed under Oz's nose. "Recognize this face?"

Oz blinked, wondering for a moment if he were dreaming. "Yeah," he finally said. "That's the Soviet that was trying to get us to give up the Superstealth."

"That's Major Sergei Federov, until a few days ago with the KGB. Seems he didn't return to Moscow after he went to Paris. Rumor has it he appeared at our Paris bureau—with some information to trade for a new identity. Everyone was a little perplexed at the fact that he didn't want any money; most of the Soviets who've defected in the past wanted money. Of course that was before the Cold War officially came to an end.

"Anyway, I understand that several million dollars are still missing from the Jouniaux estate. And apparently the industrialist had some of the money on him when he left Belgium."

"Meaning he lost the money when the Soviets tracked him down in Switzerland?"

"Well, the guy had about fifteen Soviet slugs in him when we found his corpse in the field near the wreckage. I suspect we can rule out suicide."

"So is the CIA going to get Jouniaux's money back?"

"The agency won't have anything to do with it," Grant said with a grin as he stood up. "Sounds more like a job for the international courts. In the meantime, get rested up. I have a little job for you as soon as you get up."

Oz groaned and threw a pillow at Grant as the agent quickly left the room.

Duncan Long is internationally recognized as a firearms expert, and has had over twenty books published on that subject, as well as numerous magazine articles. In addition to his nonfiction writing, Long has written a science fiction novel, *Antigrav Unlimited.* He has an MA in music composition, and has worked as a rock musician; he has spent nine years teaching in public schools. Duncan Long lives in eastern Kansas with his wife and two children.